Frank Trollope

The Rival Doctors

A novel. Part 2

Frank Trollope

The Rival Doctors
A novel. Part 2

ISBN/EAN: 9783337043964

Printed in Europe, USA, Canada, Australia, Japan

Cover: Foto ©Andreas Hilbeck / pixelio.de

More available books at **www.hansebooks.com**

THE RIVAL DOCTORS:

A NOVEL,

In Two Volumes.

By

FRANK TROLLOPE,

AUTHOR OF "A RIGHT-MINDED WOMAN;" "AN OLD MAN'S SECRET."

Vol. II.

LONDON:
T. CAUTLEY NEWBY, PUBLISHER,
30, WELBECK STEEET, CAVENDISH SQUARE·

————

1867

THE RIVAL DOCTORS.

CHAPTER I.

Willie Sawyer went on his way with a light heart, humming snatches of songs of love and war, much to his own satisfaction and the amusement of passers by, whom he eyed laughingly when they happened to be of the feminine gender. On and on he went, till he stopped at the door of the house in which his widowed cousin resided. He gave a tremendous tug at the bell, such as had not been done for many a day, and the door not being

opened quite as quickly as his hot impatience
required, he gave a thundering knock, which
brought poor dead Silverton's confidential
valet with his thin red nose, who, looking half
startled, said :—

"What may you want, sir?"

"Open the door, you snail," was the reply;
"I'm come to see, Mabel!"

The old man gazed at him with an air of
doubt and astonishment, scanning his face and
figure with great minuteness.

"Well, old fellow," laughed Sawyer,
"what do you think of me; am I not a good-
looking youth?   Come, open the door and
let me in."

"Mrs. Singleton sees no one, sir."

"Oh!" doesn't she; then the sooner she
sees me the better;" and clutching the old
servant's arm, he firmly but gently removed
his hand from the door, winked a knowing
wink, and running past him ascended the

stairs two at a time, singing one of his favorite
airs and laughing at the wondering serving
man. He made straight for the room which
he remembered as that in which his cousin
used to sit; and there he found her looking
most lovely and most feminine in her widow's
cap and black dress; working quietly, but
with a shade of melancholy on her brow;
she was thinking of her departed husband, re-
calling to memory all those kind deeds and
kinder words with which he invariably greeted
her; but there were no tears in her eyes,
though a tender sigh from time to time
escaped her. Her daughter-in-law was also in
the room pondering over her book and looking as sour as ever. Her reading and Mabel's
meditations were suddenly checked by the
jovial song ringing on the stairs, and, to their
dismay, the door flew open and in rushed
Sawyer.

"My darling Mabel!" he exclaimed, the moment he saw her, and running towards her caught her whilst hurriedly rising from her chair, folded her in an embrace worthy of a bear, and imprinted kiss after kiss upon her cheeks, which sounded fearfully in the ears of the sour old maid. Mabel was too much astonished, and her heart beat too wildly, for resistance—Barbara rose moodily from her chair, and Willie flew at her and seizing her in his arms squeezed and kissed her in the same merciless manner.

"My dear old verjuice," he cried giving her a final squeeze, whilst she struggled to free herself from his grasp, "how are you?"

"Horrible man!" shrieked Barbara, still struggling with him; he suddenly let go his hold, and she fell at his feet in a sitting posture, and so much was she taken by surprise that she remained in that position, whilst Sawyer made the room ring with his boisterous laughter, in which the gentle Mabel could not help joining.

" Come my blush rose, my tulip," Sawyer at length said, wiping his eyes, and insinuating his hands beneath her arms, " let me put you on your pins again. There, my piece of antiquity, never try to box and wrestle with a good looking young fellow when he tries to kiss you again."

Sawyer then turned and said to them both, " Now, my tulips, have the goodness to tell me who I am ? "

He pulled off his hat and placing his hand upon his breast, made then a profound bow.

" Who else can you be, but my cousin Willie," said Mabel holding out her hand " though you are stouter and browner, and your voice deeper, than when you left us; there is no mistaking you."

" Yes, Mabel, that is a few years ago, and

truly you have altered but little, and that for the better." And now let me look at you, turning to Barbara.

"'Pon my veracity I don't know what to say, my old one. Any nice looking fellows on board, eh?—Been crossed in love? eh?—how has the world wagged with you?—come, don't give a poor fellow such black looks—you shall have another squeeze if you do!"

So saying he walked towards Barbara to suit the action to the word, but the old maid threw her book at his head, which missed him, as she ran, vociferating ugly words, from the room.

"Just the same as ever, a crabbed old maid," said Sawyer, as she banged the door after her; and taking a seat close beside his cousin, they were soon absorbed, each in the relation of their respective adventures. Mabel wept a little, and Willie said all kinds of soothing and comforting words, and for the time setting aside his frolicsome humour, talked with so much tenderness, and with such friendliness, that she soon felt Brewster was not the only friend she had in the world.

Three hours had gone by, and Sawyer had risen to depart, when he bethought him of his friend Peter, and the message he was deputed to deliver.

"By the bye, Mabel," he cried, "listen to me. There is one of the handsomest fellows in the city of London, dressed in the most approved fashion, whose eyes are as tender— as tender—as a chicken, and hands as white— white as your own, salutes you through me, his confidential ambassador."

Mabel merely bowed her head, and Sawyer rattled on :

"I wanted him to be the bearer of his own message and come with me this morning, but he feared to intrude, so commissioned me, his right trusty friend and ally, to tell you so, and to say—ah ! what did he tell me to say—what

was it?" and Willie looked inside his hat as
if what he wanted was lodged there, but not
finding it, he went on in his own way·
"Bother take it, Mabel, I can't remember
what the fellow's words were,—I only know
he told me to say it would make him deuced
happy, if you would allow him to call and see
you, at any time that best suited you. That's
a sort of rough translation of the original.
Now, what shall I say to my friend in
return?"

"Willie you are as wild as ever. You
haven't told me the name of this friend of yours."

"By Jingo! no more I have. He's a first
rate fellow, I assure you. I lodge with him,
and he says you know him, and 'pon my life
he's just the lad to cheer you up."

"But his name, Willie?"

"I'll let you guess three times, so try your
hand."

"You must give some clue."

"Oh! to be sure, he's tall, handsome, well dressed, a perfect gentleman. When we were boys he was a regular dare-devil; but he has sobered down now, and yet he's a fine, manly, daring, noble-hearted fellow — come, Mabel, give guess number one."

Mabel knew but one man who answered her cousin's description, and that was Peter Jenkins, of whom she had scarcely thought since her husband's death. Now, the remembrance of him, and their walk in the green lanes, suddenly rushed to her memory, and as it did so, she blushed.

"I think," she replied, looking timidly at her cousin, "you mean Dr. Peter Jenkins."

"Ah! ah! Mabel," laughed Sawyer, "so I do. But what's the use of blushing, eh?"

Mabel turned away her head, but her incorrigible cousin seized the tip of her ear, and gently drew it back again, saying:—

" Come now, I won't plague you ; so blush like a rose, or an old woman's red cloak if you like, only tell me what to say to Jenkins. Shall I bring him with me ?   It would do you all the good in the world to see him. It's no use your being stewed up here with that sour old maid, and that ugliest of ugly beasts, Brewster, who, by your account, is the only man you see,—yes, or no,—Is he to come ? "

. " Yes," returned Mabel, " I shall be glad to see him again."

" That's right, Mabel, and now good bye, my sweet cousin."

So saying he shook hands with her, and commencing a song, began to descend the stairs. About half-way he met Brewster ascending. He stopped his song, and spreading out his arms and legs on each side, as far as they would reach, he barred the way to the mounting man.

" Why you old sinner,—you shrivelled

pear," cried Sawyer, "why, you skin flint, you are only the shadow of a daddy-long-legs. Upon my conscience, I never saw the like of you in all my travels! By Jingo! you look as if you had tried all sorts of experiments upon your lean carcase, and they every one had failed. Where are you climbing to up these stairs, you shadow of a man?"

Brewster raised his eyes at this singular salutation, but he had not the slightest remembrance of ever having seen the young man before. And to meet him singing, and shouting on Mrs. Silverton's stairs, astonished him.

"Who are you, sir? I beg you will let me pass."

"Not till you have exercised your wits and your memory, and guessed who I am, then you shall pass toll free."

"I know you not, young man, so let me pass!" exclaimed Brewster, his anger shewing itself in the tone of his voice.

"Wait a bit," said Willie gathering up his legs and arms, "I'm tired of standing like a hawk on a barn door. But I'll defend the pass, so guess away, my Apollo!" and Sawyer drew himself up and looked as fierce as he could. "Well," he continued "who am I? Satan—old Harry—old Nick, or Will-o-the-wisp? come look sharp," and Willie just touched the tip of Brewster's nose with the end of his stick. The Doctor looked perfectly demoniacal.

"It's no use urging you further. I see you cannot guess. Why, I'm an old and *valued* acquaintance of yours 'Blue Skin.' Don't you remember a refreshing ride you once took on the back of a cow; and the milk-maid who boxed your ears, and one Willie Sawyer, who kindly helped you on the cow's back, together with two other mad youths? Don't you remember now?"

"Aye, that I do," said Brewster mastering

his indignation, "why did you not tell me who you were at first. My time is precious, so let me pass."

"Let you pass! what without having guessed. No, no! you must follow me, and I will introduce you to my cousin Mabel!"

Turning round, Sawyer preceded Brewster, who followed with curses in his heart, but no words upon his lips—and on reaching Mabel's door, Sawyer sung out :—

" Here comes a man with figure lean
And ugly as the devil,—
With nose as red."

" Don't think I'm personal, Brewster,—my song can't mean you. Come along, here we are," and throwing open the door and at the same time seizing Brewster's hand, he led him forward saying: "Lovely Mabel, allow me to introduce this precious specimen of humanity, whom I met on the stairs. He's as wily old serpent as ever crawled the earth—

you must be on your guard, pretty coz, I know
him of old. He's just the man to kiss a pretty
milk-maid on the sly. He looks demure
enough, but he's wild at heart, so I'd just warn
you. Now, having done my cousinly duty,
I'll leave you—take care of your heart!—Good
bye ' Blue Skin,' " he added as he went out,
but not without clutching Brewster by both
arms, and literally twisting him round.

The door was closed, and Doctor Brewster
felt anything but satisfied, or comfortable, as
he stood fronting the widow. It was assuredly
not an agreeable method of being introduced
to the presence of a lovely woman, upon
whose heart he had a design, and it will not
be matter of surprise that his rage was
almost ungovernable as he stood without
speaking.

Mabel, however, wishing to relieve his embarrassment, stepped forward and offered him
her hand.

" I beg, Doctor Brewster, you will take no heed of my cousin's nonsense," she said in gentle tones, " he was always a wild youth ; but he intends no harm, for he has really a kind, good heart, and means not what he says. He has spent the greater part of his life in rough society, and his manners are consequently untutored. Pray, forgive him, Doctor Brewster, he ought to have been more respectful to you. His long absence and many trials, have not lowered his spirits ; he often makes me angry,—but he shews no respect to persons—he serves all alike."

" For your sake I will think no more of him or his rough manners," said Brewster in his blandest tones, " he is, as you say, young and may improve—but what does he in your house ? "

" He is my cousin, and has just returned from sea," answered Mabel. " He came to visit me, and truly glad I was to see him, for, in spite of his wildness, Willie has an exceedingly good heart, and I love him as I should a kind brother.   Moreover, he was a great favorite of my dear husband's, and I cannot forget that."

"You are always right, Mrs. Silverton," said Brewster, "your gentle heart is all kindness," and he gave her an affectionate look which caused her to cast down her eyes, with a feeling of displeasure, she knew not why.   Brewster touched her hand as he continued : " Beware, Mrs. Silverton, of your cousin, for although, as you say, he may be good at heart, he is evidently a gay, unthinking man.   No doubt, too, he is an agreeable contrast, after having been so much in the company of one so serious as I am by nature."

"Oh ! Doctor Brewster ! " interrupted Mabel, "how can you speak so to *me*.   Your company has ever been a source of comfort to me.   You have so kindly borne with me, in my sorrow, that I shall ever esteem your society.

A smile of satisfaction curled Brewster's diabolical lips, and he went on :

" I thank you with all my heart, but as I was saying, I would have you beware of your cousin. He may wind himself into your affections ; he may even introduce into your house some of his wild, reckless associates, whose manners may also be pleasing—but whose society would disgrace you: I would advise you not to allow him so much familiarity in your presence."

Mabel scarcely knew how to reply, or what to think of these words, for she could not imagine that any harm could arise from her intercourse with her merry, kind-hearted cousin. Brewster continued to say a great many things to his detriment, till Mabel at length urged :—

" He was a great favorite with my dear

husband, who was always pleased to see him and admitted him freely."

"That may be very true, dear Mrs. Silverton, but *then* you had a husband, who could shield you from harm. It is different now; you are alone in the world, with no one to protect you; cast, as it were, upon a vile world. Dear innocent lady, how my heart bleeds for you," and wiping his eyes, as if there were tears there. Brewster, added softly, " how I love you ! "

Mabel felt considerable embarrassment, from the peculiar manner in which Brewster uttered the last words; but she replied in her kindest tones.

" Oh, Doctor Brewster, I have no fear as long as I have your protection.—Will you not continue to be as a father to me ? "

" Yes, dear Mrs. Silverton," he answered, in his most persuasive accents, putting his handkerchief into his pocket, I will protect you to the utmost of my ability : but I am not always at your side, as I should be if I were your father, or your husband, to watch over you as I desire to do,—ah ! me !" A long pause ensued, neither spoke. Mabel drew a bouquet of flowers towards her, and began to re-arrange them. Her thoughts reverted to her cousin : and then, it suddenly flashed across her mind, that Sawyer would bring one of his companions to visit her, and the conviction caused her to blush. This was noticed by Brewster, and he would have given worlds to have known what induced the blush, but though he deemed it caused by his words or by his eloquent sigh, prudence prompted discretion ; so he continued silent and satisfied, but spoke not, whilst the blush deepened on Mabel's face as she recalled to her memory, how Doctor Jenkins had always been welcomed by her husband, and was highly respected by him. But Brewster's words about her unprotected state interfered with her consolation.

Mabel became anxious and fearful; and she wished to tell her companion of Doctor Jenkins' intended visit, but some undefined feeling kept her silent. Greatly embarrassed, she at length said, pushing the flowers from her :

" Dear Doctor Brewster, what am I to do ? "

Brewster hesitated a moment.

" I would recommend that in due time, not now, but when your violent grief has subsided, and your great sorrow-wound more healed,—I would recommend you to marry ! "

" I cannot."

" Not now, dear Ma——dear Mrs. Silverton, not now. Wait awhile—wait awhile. You will not cherish a vain grief, for that would be sinful, and I know you cannot do wrong. It is your duty to marry again, and to make yourself useful to your fellow creatures, as well as to give yourself a protector."

Mabel shook her head, but spoke not, and Brewster also remained silent, thinking that he had gone far enough for the present.

After a pause, Brewster arose to take his departure, but ere he went, he again impressed on Mabel's mind to be cautious how she admitted her cousin to her confidences. He shook her hand with great warmth, and as he left congratulated himself that his wily plans were prospering, and that the blush he had seen spread over Mabel's face, was produced by his sigh, instead of being called up by the sudden fears of a timid, simple minded woman.

CHAPTER II.

———

Left to her own meditations, the young widow pondered over what had passed—she thought of her cousin Willie, of her cousin's friend, of Brewster, and Brewster's words—to marry! The man to whom she had looked up to as a father, as a protector, as a counseller had advised her to marry. She was alone, young, and not in the slightest degree versed in the ways of the world, but she fondly clung to her husband's memory, and fell into a train of recollections, in which his kindness, his goodness, his tender love for her, and his death, filled her heart with gratitude, love, sorrow, and all the tender emotions. Her eyes filled with tears, and sighs left her breast as she said to herself, " marry ! no, I can never marry again, yet," she thought, " Doctor Brewster bade me wait—he is a wise man and knows better than I do, what is good for me, —but no, I can never again marry ! "

Then her thoughts roved to her cousin Willie, with a thrill of pleasure at his return, which was the next moment clouded by the wily cautions of Doctor Brewster. Then came the image of the handsome, manly looking Jenkins, and the uncertainty if she had not done wrong in omitting to mention his inten- ded visit to her on the morrow to Doctor Brewster; again she remembered that Jenkins had always been received with pleasure, and parted from with regret by her kind husband.

Then arose the recollection of their meeting in the lane; and his words and bright looks, and the pallor that overspread his countenance when they parted—and she wondered, almost before she well knew what she was wondering about, whether he still loved her! she hoped he did, and her heart beat, her color rose, and she tried to turn her thoughts into some other channel, but a thousand other forgotten circumstances, relating to Peter, rushed forward and prevented her doing so. She saw him dashing across the meadow, as the poor labourer lay bleeding on the grass, she recollected his full melodious voice, and gentle yet merry laugh, his bright eyes, his splendid figure, and above all, his kindness,—she also recollected seeing him ride past her house, frequently, saluting her courteously, and gracefully. In fact a host of slight incidents crowded her brain, all to his advantage.

The widow's heart beat wildly when the

remembered the promise Jenkins had made
her, never to come into her presence unless
asked to do it, and he had faithfully kept his
word; but he had requested for permission to
visit her now that she was free. Did he still
love her! She sighed deeply, for there was a
strange mixture in her heart of reverence for
her departed husband, and a sensation of joy
that Jenkins should have entreated an interview.

Was the widow Silverton, whose husband
had been dead only three months, in love with
Peter Jenkins?—No, she was not! She,
however, thought of him with pleasure and
increasing interest, and not having any very
important matters to occupy her time, or
attention, it must be confessed that she
passed the greater part of the day, looking
forward with curiosity and satisfaction to the
promised meeting.

The next morning Mrs. Silverton, surveyed

herself in her glass longer, and more attentively than had been her custom of late; her plain white handkerchief, was put on with much care, her hair was smoothed again and again before it pleased her, and altogether she had much greater trouble, and took much longer time than usual in adjusting the various paraphernalia; and all this labour was caused by the expected visit of Peter Jenkins, although she did not admit as much to herself, but during the time the process of dressing was going on, her thoughts were with him, and, as she mused, she touched and re-touched every article of attire, and when she had finished, she could not help thinking that she was ill-dressed.

Mabel went to her usual sitting-room alone, and as she sat there, a hope crossed her mind, that Doctor Brewster would not pay her his accustomed visit that morning; or at any rate not whilst Doctor Jenkins was with her. She had not remained long, before she heard the voice of her cousin, singing an unusually grave ditty, in fact one so unlike his usual songs, as to strike her forcibly. The air was sad and dolorous in the extreme, and instead of rushing into the room in his usual headlong manner, he came with slow and measured steps, with a face of pretended grief, and as he advanced he chaunted forth :—

"Oh sad's the hour and sad's the day,
For I and my love are parted,
We cannot meet—he's far away
And I'm almost broken-hearted!"

He gave an extraordinary and prolonged shake on the last word, and then skipped into a chair, and, taking off his hat, whilst contorting his face into a mock ludicrous melancholy state, he said :—

"Ah! me, cousin Mabel!" and drawing forth his pocket handkerchief put it to his eyes.

c 3

" Why, Willie, what's the matter ? " asked Mabel with a half smile upon her countenance, and a somewhat disappointed feeling at her heart.

" What's the matter,—why Peter Jenkins has been within a hair's breadth of crying, like a full-grown baby !—why don't you shew a little more sympathy,"

" For what ? "

" For what ! why for Peter, who has been nearly blubbering. I dare say you are dying to know what I have to tell, so just draw your chair a little nearer to mine, and I'll let you into the mystery."

Mabel drew her chair closer to her cousin.

" Now, Mabel, listen ; Jenkins and I sallied forth for the purpose of calling upon you, immediately after breakfast, that is after my breakfast, for poor Peter could not eat, and so I had to do double duty, I took no notice ; there was scarcely a word spoken, for he was

too busy with his thoughts, and I too much
engaged in devouring fish, flesh, and fowl—but
by Jove, all at once, in comes Billy with such
a well brushed beaver, such an extensive
coat, and such a cane! positively tipped with
gold! Really, coz, it almost took away my
appetite, but after a moment I managed to
replenish my plate, though it would have
grieved a saint to see Peter's countenance,
although he is generally very patient. I could
not help noticing that his eye wandered first
to the clock, and then to my plate; and then
he got up and walked about the room, every
now and then his eye wandering to my plate.
At length he was fairly beaten,—his patience
was exhausted, and would you believe it, he
asked me if I were ready to start before I had
finished my breakfast, and positively half an
hour before the appointed time, which with my
usual good nature I pointed out to him."

"He must be a very impatient man," said
Mabel naively.

"To be sure he is," replied Sawyer nodding and smiling as he continued. " Well, after awhile we started. Peter took my arm, and commenced walking at as rapid a pace as if I had eaten as little as himself. We had scarcely gone the length of the street, when on turning our heads, who should we behold but Billy, running after us without his hat at full speed, his hair standing erect, the wind fanning his flames, which stood up like a chimney on fire, and his arms going like the sails of a windmill as a signal for us to bring to."

" ' Master — master — stop ! Here be the Duke's valley, come for you ! ' cried Billy, as well as want of breath would allow him.

" ' Let him wait.' "

" ' But he can't wait – his master be dying !'

" ' He must wait," cried Peter angrily, dragging me off, I'll be back in an hour.'

" ' He'll be stone dead in an hour. The valley do say, as how the Duchess be in such a taking for you to be there ! '

"Peter didn't seem to care for duke, death, or duchess, but Billy and I forced him back, and I led him up to the very door of the Duke's house, or, by Jove, he'd have come on here without me. Upon my veracity I never saw such a disappointed man in my life."

Here Willie paused for a few minutes, during which he nodded his head significantly, staring his cousin full in the face.

"I tell you what, Mabel," he went on, "Jenkins is over head and ears in love with you, or my name's not Willie Sawyer, that's all!"

Mabel blushed, laughed, and tried to speak, but Sawyer jumped up, saying:—

"I haven't time to hear your confession just now sweet, coz, for I must be off; you may shake your head, but credit my words, Peter will make you believe so, if I cannot. I'll bring him to-morrow."

He shook her hands heartily, and giving

her a kiss on the cheek, walked to the door,
which he opened, but shut it again and returned to his cousin.

"By Jove, Mabel, I almost forgot something, I wanted to say to you, something very
particular.

"Be cautious of that sneaking, ugly scamp,
"Blue Skin."

"Blue Skin," repeated Mabel, "who is
'Blue Skin?'

"Why, Brewster—Blue Brewster, Devil
Brewster—Doctor Brewster, it's all one and the
same; be cautious of him that's a darling
Mabel."

"Doctor Brewster! caution respecting him!
why Willie I don't know what I should have
done without his kind aid, and his discreet
counsel!"

"Discreet fiddle stick! what a pretty little
donkey you are cousin. You think him discreet, aye, and so do many others besides

yourself; but I don't—I know his sneaking ways of old, and I know, too, those who know him better than I do. I have made enquiries about this paragon, and I don't like the answers I got."

"What were they, Willie?"

"Oh, bad as bad can be," replied Sawyer, "Mabel, darling, I always knew he was a hypocritical scoundrel. You have kept yourself immured up here, or you would have heard those reports about him as well as others. He has made you believe whatever he chose to tell you. It is reported he gets drunk nightly and is losing his practice daily. He will not stir from the house after dark, and his man Thomas says he is going crazy. One night Thomas heard him bellowing like a bull, and all at once he ran into his room, and dashed headlong into his bed as if lucifer was after him. His teeth chattered, and his limbs shivered, and he talked of a walking corpse of an old hag, and bleeding some fellow to death. and all sorts of stuff."

"Surely, Willie, there must be some mistake, Doctor Brewster cannot do such things."

"No, no, sweet coz, there's no mistake about the man or his wrong doings. So, now Mabel, just pay attention to what concerns yourself."

Mabel looked frightened, and Willie without noticing it, went on :—

"They say, dear Mabel, that this evil fiend. this hypocrite, has fallen over head-and-ears in love with you, and that you have been stupid enough to fall in love with him; and that he intends, at the proper season, when you can with decency leave off your widow's garments, to make you his wife, to live amongst bones, gallipots and physic."

Mabel started, and was about to make some remark, but Willie went on :—

"You may well start, but you know better

than I do whether these reports be false, or true. For my own part I do not do you the wrong of supposing you such a simpleton, and it would only be from your own lips, that I would believe. It is said, moreover, that he persuades you to remain shut up in your house to make more sure of you— to keep you from other influence. Peter Jenkins must ferret all this out. Now tell me, do you really love that vile, parched up piece of humanity, or do you not? "

"Love him, Willie! No, not in the way that you have been told—I love him, or rather respect him, as lately my best friend and counseller; but I do not believe he has——" here she paused, as sudden remembrances flashed into her mind, and forced upon her his words, his modulated tones and tender looks; she paused and blushed.

" That will do, my darling cousin," said Sawyer, " look sharply after him, and trust to

me, scapegrace, as I am, or as Peter calls me,
rather than to Brewster, sanctimonious as he
appears. You will find me honest and truthful as the open day, he's as dark, and hidden,
as an underground cavern. Now, good bye,
keep up your spirits, and you shall see Peter
Jenkins, in his well brushed beaver, his
fashionable cut coat, and his cane tipped with
gold, please the weather and his patients."

Willie made a jump over one of the chairs,
and went towards the door, which at the
moment opened to admit the widow's step-
daughter

"Oh, you pretty little darling," cried
Willie in an endearing tone, "dear, tender little
duck—light of my life, bundle of sweet odours,
give me a kiss!" he seized, and, in spite of
screams and cuffs, kissed her, took her up
in his arms, ran with her into the room, and
with a loud laugh deposited her on the table,
full length; and then went away singing at

the top of his voice, whilst she flounced off the table on to her feet screaming:

"Mabel, Mabel, how can you permit such a monster as that to come into your presence. If you associate with such a cracked demon, you cannot expect that I should remain any longer in the same house with you," and she smoothed her ruffled dress, and bounced out of the room to the delight of her step-mother, who wanted to be alone, to indulge in undisturbed reflection upon what she had heard. She felt certain. her cousin knew nothing of what had passed between Doctor Jenkins and herself when they had last parted, but Willie guessed rightly, that he loved her. Mabel felt the truth of her cousin's assertion and she was pleased. Willie's words, too, that she would one day be Peter's wife; and Brewster's advice to her to marry, flashed across her mind. Then, came the thought of her husband's kindness and tenderness. Had she analysed

her feelings, she would easily have discovered
the reason why, though she loved and regretted
him as fondly as ever, the idea of a marriage
with the handsome Doctor, no longer startled
her. She had loved her husband with a love very
different from that, which, without her suspec-
ting it, was even then taking root in her heart
for another. The two feelings could very well
exist together, without being in actual opposi-
tion.

The ideas of a young mind are not very
firmly fixed, a breeze will blow away one set,
and blow up another in their place. There is
no argument, no battle necessary to change
before age firmly fixes them. Thus Mabel's
thoughts, ere the day closed, were scudding
away before the breath of Willie's words, and
another set taking their places. His account
of Brewster was reviewed by her. She recollected the said Brewster's looks, looks which
had, at the time, puzzled and displeased her.

—Could it be possible that he loved her?—
Then Sawyer had named such strange things
about him, had called him a hypocrite—could
it be? Mabel was somewhat credulous and
this very credulousness induced in her some
belief in her cousin's words; then occurred
Brewster's cautions about that very cousin,
and she became greatly embarrassed. She
could not compare, search out, analyze, deduce,
or form from such proceedings a conclusion; she
was one of those persons who hear and believe,
provided what they hear is not outrageously
preposterous; and now she had heard, and she
believed each by turns. At length she commenced her work, and attended to her
domestic duties, every now and then the image
of Jenkins, thrusting itself in, and bringing
with it hourly more pleasing reflections, whilst
that of Brewster, she could not say why,
became almost revolting in spite of all his kind
attentions, consolation and advice.

Brewster love her! such a monstrous absur-
dity had never once entered her imagination,
but now that her cousin had introduced it
there—she began to feel a horror of the man
creeping over her, which she could not,
neither did she try to control. She did not
dislike him, for Mabel was incapable of that
passion, but when she thought of him, a species
of shuddering came over her, and she dreaded
his again coming to see her. Her meditations
were interrupted by the entrance of a servant,
bringing a note, which was written in a very
cramped hand: It was from Brewster, and
was as follows:—

" Dear Mrs. Silverton,

"I regret, very much regret,
that I cannot, as I had intended and wished,
pay you my accustomed visit to-day. This is
grief to me, real grief. But please Heaven I
will be with you to-morrow. In the mean-
time I would have you remember the words of

warning I gave you yesterday, for they were
the words of a loving friend. Beware of
wolves! I would watch over you as a husband
or father, for I am anxious for your welfare,
day and night. We will again talk over your
peculiar situation.

" Believe me,

"My dear Mrs. Silverton,

"Your devoted friend,

"J. Brewster."

The word husband in this short epistle displeased Mabel, and she threw the note into
the fire and watched it, till it was burnt, and
she saw the burnt remnants fly up the chimney.
She then dismissed, all thought of Brewster for
the present, and amused herself with more
pleasing meditations.

CHAPTER III.

The following morning Mabel underwent the same process in her toilette as she had done the previous day, and with more satisfaction to herself. So she proceeded to her sitting room full of pleasant anticipations. In due time Sawyer's voice was heard carolling a more cheerful song than on the previous day. The door was opened and Sawyer entered the room, saying:

"Here we are, my darling Mabel: Arise! arise! lay by your work and put on your most loving smile to receive the urbane, captivating, and most able Doctor Peter Jenkins, together with his trusty ally one Master Willie Sawyer, the most gentlemanly man in the city of London, slim as a fishing rod, and quiet as a sleeping baby. Doctor Peter Jenkins, thou caressed and petted of the noble of the land, walk in, you life destroying leech, walk in, and make your most courtly bow to this lovely and angelic lady—and both of you renew your acquaintance at the very point where it was snapped in twain. Make yourselves at home, do not stand upon ceremony, don't think about me !"

Mabel did arise and smile, and Peter Jenkins did enter and made his obeisance. Mabel blushed when Willie spoke of renewing their acquaintance and Peter smiled, but with his accustomed taste and good feeling withdrew his eyes from her face so that he might not embarrass her.

"I can assure you, Mrs. Silverton," said Peter, "I feel a most lively pleasure in renewing our intimacy. I should long since have asked permission to call upon you, but I feared to intrude. Besides I heard that you saw no one, and it is only owing to my fortunate encounter with your cousin, who was my playmate in our early days, that I now have the happiness of visiting you."

"I am very pleased to see you, Doctor Jenkins" replied Mabel, and although they were the only words she spoke, the tone and manner convinced Peter of his welcome, and he held out his hand in his cordial manner, and it instantly received that of the young widow, which trembled slightly, but which she hoped Jenkins did not perceive. She however, was deceived, Peter did perceive it, and it gave him great pleasure.

Sawyer winked behind Peter's back at his

dress and cane, and then placing a chair said :

" Come, sit down Jenkins, you have a large amount of business to transact before you go. You are not going to pay a doctor's ten minutes' visit, feel a pulse, inspect a tongue, I suppose by way of measuring it for a dose, then look grave, and after putting out your hand for the fee make your exit. No, no, Doctor Peter Jenkins, this must be quite a different sort of visit."

" Sawyer, Sawyer, you are enough to alarm Mrs. Silverton," said Peter laughing, "you are a merry fellow but unfit for a gentle lady."

" Oh, don't alarm yourself, Peter; my little rose-bud of a cousin knows me of old, so, sit you down, and just pay attention to me whilst I give you a rapid sketch of your duties."

" I am all attention," replied Peter with a smile, taking the seat Willie had placed for him, "and shall be only too happy if I can in any way be of service to Mrs. Silverton."

"Thank you," said Mabel, also smiling.

"Bravo, bravo," cried Willie, laughing and clapping his hands; and jumping over a chair his hat flew off his head and in its descent rolled among the ashes in the fire-place; dashing after it he seized it only just in time to prevent a burning piece of wood falling on it, and placing the hat on the table he seated himself and said :

"Doctor Peter Jenkins, I brought you here that you might free my cousin Mabel and this house of a foul fiend by which they are infested. I have seen the fiend. It is blue and black, has a lanky visage and a look sour enough to turn the milk in all the dairies in Suffolk. It is plausible, hypocritical, wicked, devilish . . It is——"

"Oh! Willie, Willie, dear," interrupted Mabel, "I beg you——"

" Oh! Mabel, Mabel dear," interrupted
Willie imitating his cousin's voice and manner. "I beg you, hear me out—Peter, this
vile thing considers himself at liberty to haunt
this house at all hours, looking as sanctified as
a Puritan parson, and he has persuaded my little cousin to mew herself up and only listen to his
hypocritical sayings, causing her spirits to flag
—and—and—shall I, Mabel, eh, shall I ? "

" Shall you what, Willie ? " cried Mabel,
" Doctor Jenkins is ashamed of you, and—"

" And—and— here goes," said Willie, " He
wants this gentle fawn to fall in love with him
and become Mrs.——"

" Willie, Willie, dear, stay, I entreat you."
Mabel looked agitated, and Peter was at a loss
to know whether it was the agitation of consciousness or not.

" Sawyer, my merry friend, your exuberant
spirits carry you at times beyond proper bounds.
You are distressing, Mrs. Silverton."

"Poor dear little trembling dove," said
Willie "it can't be helped, but I'll cut my
story as short as possible. The fiend is ' Blue
Skin,' and I want you to turn him out neck
and crop, and if Mabel wants a man of medi-
cine, why the best thing she can do, is at once
to take you into her confidence."

"Mrs. Silverton may not be inclined to ask
me to take so much upon myself. On the
contrary she may, perhaps, give Doctor
Brewster the power to do the same by me."

"Not she, I'll be sworn," said Willie.

"Doctor Jenkins," said Mabel gravely,
" after what my cousin has said it is right
that I should speak in my turn."

" Indeed, Mrs. Silverton, I give little heed
to Sawyer's nonsense. I know him for an idle
wag. Let not his madness and idle words
distress you."

" Madness ! Idle wag ! marry come up,

what next, Peter. Oh! sad's the day and sad's the hour." he sung out, "that I should live to hear such accusations."

"Yes, idle words," said Jenkins, "so let your good cousin speak, and if you can, do you listen for awhile."

"Doctor Jenkins," said Mabel, whilst Sawyer closed his eyes, pursed up his mouth and twiddled his thumbs, "my cousin would, I fear, give you a wrong impression. It is true that Doctor Brewster has been often with me. He was much esteemed by my husband and I have been greatly indebted to him for kind counsel and consolation since I have been left alone. I cannot but feel very grateful to one so very kind, but Willie's insinuations are——"

Mabel hesitated, and averted her eyes, and Jenkins spoke :

"I quite understand your feelings, Mrs.

Silverton, and believe me I esteem you all the more, they are worthy of you."

" Under your favor," said Willie, opening his eyes " he is too much here. Neighbours begin to talk." He closed his eyes again as if he desired to listen.

" We will not say another word upon the subject," said Jenkins, " I think I fully understand the nature of the case. But——," he continued, with a slight hesitation, " but —— might I be allowed for the sake of the man you were so loved by, for the sake of my worthy friend poor Mr. Silverton, might I for his sake presume to say one word to you ? "

" With all my heart, Doctor Jenkins ; words so introduced can be but for my good."

A gleam of joy shone in Peter's face, which immediately gave way to a soft and tender gaiety as he said :

" You are lone and unprotected, Mrs. Silverton, and you are unacquainted with all the malicious slanderings and whisperings that go on around you. I pay little heed to Sawyer's inuendos and hints, but I would advise you to be circumspect, and not to receive too frequent visits even from Doctor Brewster, grave though he be. People will talk, and in spite of your innocence your actions will be canvassed."

Mabel blushed, turned pale and sighed.

"I hope I have not caused you pain" said Peter "I spoke from my heart and for your welfare, which, believe me, is very dear to me"

This was uttered warmly and frankly, with an open, manly expression of countenance very different from the smooth, oily, hidden manner in which Brewster had uttered nearly the same words and to the same effect.

Mabel gratefully thanked and assured him she fully appreciated his kind intentions, and that his advice would not be given in vain.

" So far, so good," cried Willie, jumping up.
Now business is over, suppose we talk of other
matters. Master Peter, try and entertain my
poor little cousin with some cheerful discourse.
You have both a winning tongue and a pleasant manner, and it will be a godsend to her,
after having been so long mewed up with those
old dolorous ravens, Barbara and Blue Skin.
She terribly wants cheering up. So let the sunshine burst in on her gloom, that is to say, do
you entertain her in your best style, and I'll
help you—I'll fill up pauses and sing her a
song, keep us all alive, and send ' Blue Skin,'
and dull care " all down below."

Mabel and Jenkins could but laugh; Peter
entertained the widow in his best manner,
whilst her air of gentle approbation and delight
gave him additional animation, and as Willie
did his part to perfection, the three became
merry and happy; Peter in being so near
Mabel and using every effort to please her;

Mabel in being so pleased; and Willie in witnessing their happiness; and singing, laughing and noting down in his mind, there existed not the slightest doubt his friend loved his cousin, and that sooner or later his cousin would love his friend.

Willie was in the seventh heaven, and was rolling forth, in his fine full-toned voice, some scrap of song *àpropos* to some part of their conversation, and snapping his fingers and clapping his hands in chorus, when the door was thrown open and in walked Dr. Brewster.

Sawyer and Jenkins, whose backs were towards the door, did not see the apparition, but Jenkins, whose eyes were fixed on Mabel, saw her change countenance, and, turning in the direction of her eyes, beheld the gaunt figure of the Doctor standing in the door-way, surprise, vexation, and anger struggling in his demonaical visage with the composure that was trying to take up its place there :—

Jenkins arose and Sawyer breaking off his chorus turned round.

"Oh glorious hour!" he cried, "oh! the happy moment! Behold the phœnix of mirth —the glory of London, the love of the ladies, the rose of summer! Walk in phœnix of mirth—glory of London, love of the ladies, rose of summer, all wrapped up in a dingy cloak, and take your place among us!"

Brewster advanced and gravely saluting the trio said to Mabel :—

"I was not aware, Mrs. Silverton, that Doctor Jenkins had the honor of being one of your acquaintances."

This was quietly said, but his eyes, he felt were looking sinister, and he prudently covered them with his hand.

Mabel knew not what to say, and Jenkins replied for her :—

"I have had that honor some time, Brewster. Were you not aware of it till the present moment? I was upon terms of intimacy with her good husband, Mr. Silverton, and he was kind enough to honor me with his especial favor."

The conversation which had been so pleasing and caused so much happiness, received a death-stab by Brewster's arrival, at least as far as Mabel and Peter were concerned, for Brewster's demeanour cast a gloom over them, which they tried in vain to shake off; whilst Sawyer, with his usual noisy want of tact, went on laughing and talking, making Brewster his butt, every now and then cutting him to his very soul; that worthy the while, though almost bursting with rage, endeavouring to preserve an appearance of equanimity and placidity, clenching his hands in his breast, and grinning what he intended should be a meek smile.

"Come, Peter," said Willie rising, and putting his hand on Jenkins' shoulder. "You

are no doubt very agreeably engaged, but I
have received an inward warning, that it is
very nearly the dinner hour; I am as hungry
as a famished beggar, and thirsty as a hound
after hunting; and as you give gloriously good
cheer, let us say good bye for the present,—
and we've been here nearly two hours—it's
'Blue Skin's' turn now. You shall come
again another time, so tear yourself away and
hasten to dinner lest the cook should let all
spoil, because we kept it waiting."

Jenkins arose, shook hands with Mabel, and
received a glance and a smile not easily to be
forgotten; then shaking hands with Brewster,
who went through the ceremony very credi-
tably, he bowed to his fair hostess and left the
room.

Willie kissed his cousin on both cheeks, and
giving Brewster a slap on the back that nearly
annihilated him, he winked at him, and following his friend, leaving Mabel to a *tête-à-tête*

with her sinister admirer. Brewster was not
a man to suffer himself to be daunted by any
circumstance, however embarassing or disa-
greeable, wherefore by the time Willie's
boisterous mirth had died away on the stairs,
he had prisoned his malignant sentiments in
the lowest depths of his heart, so that they
were prevented peering through his eyes; and
having gravely possessed himself of Mabel's
hand, as though he intended to feel her pulse,
he assumed an air of sanctimonious stiffness,
and spoke. His doing so was a relief to his
listener, for she was sadly perplexed what to
say, and although innocent knew not where
to cast her eyes save on the floor.

"My very dear Mrs. Silverton," Brewster
began. " I beg you will attribute what I say to
the anxious tenderness I feel for your welfare;
I can assure you, your happiness is more dear
to me than my own. You must be cautious,
indeed you must. I told you to beware of your

cousin, for I felt convinced he would introduce
into your house, some of his licentious companions—and he has done so, my words have
too truly come to pass.   Oh! Mrs. Silverton,
Mrs. Silverton, if you did but know my anxiety
for you, if you did but know the man who has
been talking to you, did you but guess half
his profligacy, his worthlessness, his vanity,
you would shudder at having had him seen to
enter your house, and having had him so near
you!"

Brewster paused, shook his head mournfully,
slightly pressed Mabel's hand, and then
releasing it, drew forth his pocket handkerchief,
and put it to his eyes for a minute.

Poor Mabel felt very like a naughty child,
and spoke in the piteous tones of one who
timidly feared having done wrong.

"I may have been wrong, Doctor Brewster,
but I never heard the slightest dispraise of
Doctor Jenkins. My poor husband liked him

and was always most anxious for his com-
panionship, and ever encouraged his visiting
at our house. I am very much surprised
that he should never have spoken to you about
him."

"Do not longer deceive yourself, dear Mrs.
Silverton, Jenkins is a hypocrite, a vain
coxcomb, and a cunning cheat. He knows
well how to suit himself to those, with whom
he converses. He can put on a frank and
courteous air; he can make himself appear
honest and upright, with those that are honest
and upright; and he can win hearts for the
purpose of his own devilish desires. He
suspects that you are wealthy, and he is over-
whelmed with debts. He thinks to marry
you, and his only wish in making you his
wife, would be to squander your money to
free him from his debts, and enable him to
commence anew, his days and nights of profligacy!"

" But Doctor Brewster," said Mabel s'mply
" I have not the slightest notion that he would
have me for a wife."

" So you think, poor innocent lady ! but I
know him and his arts better. All his
practice in his profession, is among rakes.
His friends are one and all the most dissolute
men about town—men whose sole end and aim
in life is rioting and gaming. Jenkins spends
all he earns by his profession, and more, in
gambling and debauchery. It is a well
known fact, that he has for some time past
been looking out for a lady of fortune to enable
him to repair his bankrupt condition; but he
is too well known by the evil living people
with whom he associates to find a wife among
them ; but you—he has determined to make you
his victim--he will use every artifice, all his
powers of fascination to induce you to become
his wife, and then destroy your happiness for
ever ! "

All this was uttered with such an air of pity and interest, that the poor widow was at a loss what to say or what to think.

"Oh! my dear Doctor Brewster," she at length cried, "can it be possible that men can be so cruelly wicked—oh! why did I not die with my poor dear husband? What shall I do—what shall I do?"

Brewster again took her hand, and putting his thin lips close to her ear, whispered "marry, dear Mabel."

He kissed her hand, and before she could recover from the surprise, she stood alone, and the gaunt form of Brewster was hurrying through the streets on the road home.

Mabel seated herself, and took her work in her hand, but not a stitch did she add to it, for her fingers were idle, but her thoughts flew through her brain with a rapidity that startled her, and the result was the most conflicting contest of opinions.

It was impossible that she should not be pleased with Jenkins. It was long since she had seen anything half as bright as his smile, or heard anything approaching his cheering and agreeable conversation, which had been kind, gentle, merry, and somewhat tender, whilst his winning, courteous manner had won her to his side. Then again, like a true woman, she had not over-looked his exquisite taste in dress, which showed off his fine, and handsome figure to the best advantage. Peter Jenkins' visit was to her, in fact, like the sun bursting through a long continued gloom of clouds, but then the thought of that bright sun was over-shadowed from time to time, by the clouds which Brewster's conversation caused to flit across it. Could it be possible that Peter Jenkins, seemingly so frank, so courteous, so kind, with a countenance open and manners so gracious and so manly, could it be possible that he was the riotous gam-

bling, sinful man, that Brewster had described
—could he be so designing—such a knave?
Was it possible that her dear husband could
have been so deceived in a man he so respected, and in whose society he felt such
pleasure—would he not have penetrated such
vileness! Mabel's heart which was simple,
truthful and upright, spurned all she had
heard, and chose to judge by what she had
seen, and she decided that Jenkins was all
that he seemed to be, and her innocent mind
directed her aright. She was convinced that
Doctor Brewster had been deceived by false
reports.

She recapitulated the conversation with
Peter Jenkins, and remembered that not a
word had he uttered against Brewster: that
he had only warned her to act with circum-
spection and discretion; and when she remembered the kind, gentle way in which he had
spoken, her heart warmed towards him. Her

thoughts then wandered to Brewster,—she
knew not what to think of him. The heart
that pleaded for Jenkins intinctively began to
warn her against his rival. She almost feared
Willie's words were true, and if Brewster
really intended seeking her as his wife, her
soul revolted at the bare idea of such treachery.
She shuddered, as she thought of the words,
whispered in her ear, "marry, dear Mabel,"
and the kiss, and looking at the little white
hand, resting on her black dress, she passed
the other over it, as if to efface that odious
kiss, — throwing herself, in idea, upon
Peter Jenkins for protection ; and as the bright
animated looks of Peter floated before her
mind, she thought that if she must marry,
she hoped that——and there the thought
broke off—as yet she dared not pursue it
further.

CHAPTER IV.

From his earliest childhood, Doctor Brewster could not, if he had traced back his feelings, have remembered to have been conscious of possessing any of a calm and pleasing description, unmixed with gall and bitterness, untinged with spleen and dissatisfaction. All his impulses had been evil and as a matter of course unhappy, and now they were more so than ever.

He walked or rather ran through the streets, his heart full of the most vindictive passions, both against Jenkins and Sawyer, and extremely angry with the widow Silverton. As to poor Willie, he cursed him with all his heart.

Rumour, with its hundred tongues, had spoken correctly about him. He had become restless and nervous in the extreme. The visions that had so beset him had taken such hold upon his imagination as to influence all his actions to the great injury of his profession and reputation. Whatever might be the urgency of a professional case, he could never be induced to go to a patient after daylight had disappeared, for latterly whenever he ventured out after sunset, his mind was filled with such horrid visions that he returned home in a most wretched condition.

At length the neighbours began to make all sorts of remarks.

" I can't think what has come over Doctor Brewster," said his butcher to the minister of the chapel he frequented. "He refuses to budge an inch after dark, let his patients require him ever so much. I verily believe Satan has got possession of his wits."

"Surely, surely" returned the minister, fixing his eyes on a fine haunch of mutton that was hanging before him. "Truly that's a splendid haunch—Satan may possess poor Brewster or he may not—but he nevertheless may persuade him to indulge in strong drinks —My mouth positively waters at that joint— He may have been guilty of some sin which now lacerates his breast—You may send me home that mutton—It would be quite out of the question to employ him when you are sick —It would be but right to make all your customers acquainted with what I have just said —Good day. Don't forget to send me the haunch."

The butcher had a large connection and to

one and all he met, he made use of the minister's words.

" I don't like to send for Doctor Brewster " said a grocer to his daughter, after a conversation with the butcher " Your mother is too seriously ill to be trifled with. I don't at all like those freaks of frenzy and craziness. What think you, my dear ? "

" I should send for Doctor Jenkins " was the prompt reply.

" But he is not of our party," returned the father.

" What has party to do with it, when my dear mother's life is in such jeopardy. Doctor Jenkins is a discreet and a clever man, and his character stands well in the city."

Jenkins was sent for and his kind and courteous manners were liked both by the mother and daughter; and his skill proving successful in curing his patient, he obtained not only their respect and confidence, but was recommended by them to a large number of persons belonging to the dissenting body who had hitherto been Brewster's patients.

"What do you call that?" cried a man who occupied a small lodging at the back of Brewster's house, starting up in his bed in the middle of that night, after Jenkins had called on the widow for the first time since her husband's death.

The man's wife also was aroused and sat up in bed by her husband's side, and both listened attentively. They heard cries and moans of the most piteous description, evidently very near, and as if wrung from some person enduring great bodily or mental suffering, and coming as those cries did through the stillness of night, they sounded doubly awful to the man and woman who trembled violently.

The husband left his bed, opened the window, and after listening for a minute, said. "The sounds come from Doctor Brewster's; I'll be bound he's cutting up some poor creature, in the dead of the night! The infamous hypocrite! No wonder he looks so wild and careworn! What shall we do?"

"What shall we do?" repeated the wife "why do you come into bed again; or you'll catch your death of cold. Shut the window — shut the window; I can't bear to hear them horrid shrieks!"

"Mercy! mercy!" pealed through the air.

The man again put his head out of the window.

"The scoundrel!" he cried, sufficiently loud to be heard by a person who was passing underneath the window.

"What is it?" asked the man from the street.

"Why, it's my belief, that methodistical surgeon is cutting up somebody before being dead!"

" Where does the surgeon live? "

" In the next street."

" Oh ! that's Dr. Brewster's house. I should think he's not the man to do that kind of thing," and the stranger laughed. " But are you sure the cries come from Doctor Brewster's house ? "

" Sure as I'm alive."

" I'll just go round and ascertain the cause Good night, my friend, you had better turn into your warm bed, or you'll be the next victim to be operated upon." The speaker was Willie Sawyer who, with his usual good nature, promised to come back and let the old couple know what was going on, and he began singing and laughing by turns.

On reaching Brewster's house he found two or three persons standing at the door whispering and listening. The cries and moans became so loud that they held a consultation as to the expediency of demanding admittance and seeking an explanation.

Sawyer, however, did not deem it necessary to consult those near him, but gave a thundering knock at the door; and waiting a couple of minutes without any one coming at his summons, he thundered again in a manner that must convince those within he was determined to have his demand for admittance attended to. He succeeded, for in another minute the door was unbolted and slowly opened, and Thomas with a lighted candle in his hand demanded, in a surly voice:

"What do you want?"

"Want," cried Sawyer. "Why we want to know, what's the cause of all those yellings and hootings and moanings that are going on in your house, disturbing all the good people in the neigbourhood and preventing them having their proper snoozing."

" You do, do you ; why then find out ; " and Thomas attempted to shut the door in Sawyer's face.

" That's what I intend to do, my fine fellow," cried Willie, preventing the shutting of the door, " and if you don't tell us what all these devilries mean, and what is the cause of all these shrieks and moanings, got up by your skin-and-grief master, these gentlemen and I will use force—so just be alive and tell us all about it."

The bystanders gave authority to this speech by drawing close to the door.

" Well, then, if you must know," cried Thomas savagely, " Master's very ill; that's all. So be off with you, poking your noses into people's houses at dead of night."

Thomas again tried to close the door, but Willie's strength was too great for him to succeed.

" Hush !" cried one of the bystanders.

VOL. II.   E

All kept silence. The cries for help came louder and louder.

"Save me! save me!" rang through the house in tones of intense agony. The sounds ceased for a moment; then came a yelling shout, and again a silence; but the next moment quick steps were distinctly heard rushing along the passage towards the door, Thomas turned; Sawyer pushed it open and Brewster, with no covering upon him but his night-shirt, ran into the street.

The bystanders drew back in affright. It appeared as if a figure from the grave had suddenly risen before them; the bright moon never shed its light upon a more cadaverous skeleton looking man. His eyes were bloodshot, his hair literally stood on end, and terror, intense terror, was stamped upon every feature of his face; his eyes rolled fearfully, but no sound issued from his lips, and he fled as if pursued by some one seeking his life.

Willie Sawyer was the only one of the party who seemed to have his wits about him. At any other time the figure of Brewster would have induced a laugh, but in the present instance his mirth gave way to action.

" After him, gentlemen! give him chase; seize him and bring him back."

Away went the party in hot chase, and Sawyer followed at his best pace, none of the swiftest, whilst Thomas, knowing they would bring back their game, closed the door and went to his room to dress himself, not omitting to take a draught from a bottle of brandy he found in his master's room.

Brewster continued his course through the deserted streets, followed by his pursuers; they gained rapidly upon him, till at length he heard the tramp of their footsteps; he turned his head and saw the withered hag joining in the pursuit, her bony arms thrown aloft, her white hair streaming in the wind and her haggard face and lustreless eyes grinning hideously and derisively at him. Suddenly his strength left him, and with a fearful cry he stood still, panting and every limb quivering. The persons in pursuit speedily surrounded the wretched man, and Sawyer, coming up, seized him by the arm.

Brewster muttered incoherently and strove to get free. He thought himself in the grasp of the hag, he imagined that her damp unwholesome breath was on his cheeks and that he heard her gibberish threats.

"I never will, I never will," he cried shivering from head to foot, " do your worst —do your worst, you grinning devil—she shall be mine—I will never give her up to another. Let go your clasp. Begone, I say, I will never give her up. Never, never, never."

His teeth chattered, and the quivering of his limbs increased.

" Come, Brewster," said Sawyer, " you are
making a pretty fool of yourself. Come home,
you'll catch such a cold as your physic will be
unable to cure ; so come along, march ! "

Brewster stared at the speaker, heaved a
deep sigh, and would, had not one of the
spectators caught him, have fallen to the
ground.

" Hallo ! neighbours," shouted the man
who had caught him in his arms. " It is Dr.
Brewster ! and all the tales I have lately heard
about him must be true. He's either mad or
mad drunk, I can't exactly say which."

" Come, gentlemen," said Sawyer, " we
must get him home, he will perish of cold if
he remains longer here. Brewster, rouse
yourself, don't be an ass."

" Why, Sir, he's fainting—he can't stand
upon his legs."

" That's true enough," returned Sawyer,

laughing, then we must carry him. Come, gentlemen lend a hand."

Brewster was carried back to his own door.

"Thank you, gentlemen," said Sawyer, "I wish you all good night—I am a friend of Doctor Brewster's, and will see him safe to bed."

The strangers commenting on what they had witnessed, took their leave, and Sawyer having knocked vigorously at the door, Thomas made his appearance.

"Help me to carry your master to his room," said Sawyer.

"Who be you?" demanded Thomas, when they had placed the unconscious Brewster on the bed.

"I am an old freind of Doctor Brewster's. Is he often thus? What is the matter with him?"

"Can't exactly say, but he's crazy I should

think. I shan't stand his vagaries much longer, I can tell you. All day long he's as cross as two sticks, with a face as black as a thundercloud, and he's as timid as a hare. And as to the nights, for the last three weeks he's kicked up such a row, when he ought to be asleep, as never was heard afore, but he's never been as bad as he's been to-night."

" Does he drink ? " asked Sawyer.

" Why, not exactly ; he doesn't drink except when he gets bedevill'd very bad, then to be sure he do take a draught or so to strengthen himself, that's all. At any rate he's quiet now, and if you don't object, I'll just show you the way out and I'll get to bed again."

" You had better remain here and watch him, my good fellow," said Willie.

" Umph ! I don't think that's necessary," said Thomas, "if he kicks up a row again, I shall be sure to hear him. I don't think he will though, he's done enough for to-night."

"Well, I suppose you know best. When he wakes, tell him William Sawyer brought him home. Good night. You must show me the way and light me out of this hole of a place."

On waking the next morning Brewster's mind was a complete chaos. He had only a very indistinct recollection of what had passed. He was extremely nervous and totally unable to attend to any of his professional duties. A settled gloom took possession of him and his thoughts were of the most harrowing description. The widow Silverton was the only idea that gave the least ray of light to his darkened mind, and that was connected with all that was horrible.

Thomas had not neglected the injunction to tell his master who had brought him home. Brewster felt a violent tornado of rage take possession of him; being perfectly certain that not only would all that had occurred be reported to

Mabel, but that it would be decorated and enlarged upon by all Sawyer's sportive talent, and that he should be literally held up to ridicule, in presence of the woman he had taken such undue pains to win. He walked up and down the room like a chafed tiger in its cage, his arms thrown to and fro, like the sails of a wind-mill; his lank face was unshaved, his teeth were firmly set, and his disorderly dress giving him the appearance of a maniac. His steps were at length arrested by a knock at the door. He called in a fierce tone, " come in," with his eyes, however, intently fixed on the door, which, on opening, gave entrance to Thomas. " What do you want? " almost roared Brewster.

Thomas stuck his arms a-kimbo, and stood doggedly before his master.

" What do I want," he returned, " why I want to know if it be your intention to kick

up such a rout every night of your crazy life;
'cause of it be I'd just have you to understand
at once, I don't intend to stay and listen to it.''

" How dare you—"

" How dare I—why do you think I'll stay
here for people to set me down, as being as
mad as yourself,—why, you've no idea what
questions people ask me about you, and the
horrid things they say of you."

Brewster's countenance became red, and
livid by turns, at these words—and it would
be utterly impossible to describe his looks
of rage, shame, terror and entreaty. At length
he spoke.

" Hold your impudent tongue; and get on
with your work. I don't know which is the
worst, you for listening, or the empty headed
fools who talk to you."

" I can't say which be the worst—but this
I can tell you—I don't intend doing a single

bit of work again in this house, till I've got an understanding with you."

"What do you mean? Get out of the room!"

"What do I mean? Why I mean that you shall double my wages to begin with!"

"Double your wages—I shall do nothing of the kind."

"Oh, very well then, I'll just quit your service, and spread about the town all I have learnt in your ravings; I'll tell of all your vagaries."

"My vagaries—my ravings?"

"Yes, and I just give you half an hour to consider about the matter—if I continue to serve you, you must double my wages, so just make up your mind and let me know."

And having had his say, Thomas left the room, leaving Brewster to think over the conversation.

"I cannot part with the fellow," he soliloquised, I would rather treble his wages than allow him to talk over my affairs; I feel that I am in his power—that he has heard more than I could wish," and he fretted terribly, walking about the room in an almost frantic state :—

At the given time Thomas re-entered.

" Well, be it a bargain ?" asked Thomas, staring his master full in the face.

" Yes, I'll double your wages."

Thomas looked a most irritating look, which Brewster resented by striking him with all his strength.

" Come, come, let's have none of that, or I'll tell you and every body else what I know about poor old Silverton! " and Thomas looked at Brewster defiantly.

Brewster gave a start, as if he had received a sudden wound, and clenching his fist, he cried menacingly.

" Scoundrel ! what do you mean ? "

"Mean; just what I say. I'll tell the whole secret of the poor old gentleman's death."

"Pshaw! man, what can you know about his death, excepting that he is dead? Who put such silly notions into your head!"

"Why, nobody, except Doctor Brewster!" returned Thomas, grinning in a most irritating manner, and Brewster cried:—

"Liar!"

"I tell you, you did. In your ravings you let out everything: how you doted on the lovely widow—how you did bleed the poor old man, till he died—and how you saw his ghost—and some old hag, and other things of the sort. Oh! Lord! I wish you could have seen yourself, staring and grinning, and bellowing, and playing off such antics."

Brewster, with a groan, threw himself into the nearest chair; and for a minute was unable to utter a word; at length he gasped forth:—

" Thomas, as you love your life—I pray you—I beseech you—speak not of——"

" I can't say what I shall do," replied Thomas leaving the room.

Brewster jumped up and seized his servant by the arm.

" Paws off! Doctor, paws off! or I may let you know which is the better man of the two. Get you back to your den, and hand out thirty crowns, and don't be in such a child's fright."

Brewster went back into the room, opened his desk, and gave the required sum to Thomas, cowering beneath the eye of his servant, who took the money and left the room.

The miserable man, again threw himself into the chair, rage, agitation, fear terrifying him by turns. He felt that he was in the power of his servant, a hard, dogged man, who had served him well enough, when he possessed no power over him, and to whom Brewster had played the tyrant, but who now was about to reverse the order of things, exulting to revenge himself, for all the insults and wrongs his master had done him.

Brewster's love of money could only be equalled by Thomas's—and it was clear enough that instead of the Doctor bleeding his servant, the servant would bleed the Doctor, and Brewster in an agonizing fit of despair made up his mind that he must submit to constant pulls upon his purse.

Then recurred the horrid conviction that Mabel would have all his last night's vagaries put before her, in the most ridiculous point of view, by Willie Sawyer. Peter Jenkins also was not forgotten, and his insinuating manners caused an additional pang: after all that he (Brewster) had done, all the trials he had undergone, Mabel might slip through his fingers, and become the wife of his detested rival! all these thoughts, rushing through his brain maddened him, and they were in truth, enough to madden any man.

Brewster was at a loss, in what way to act under the distressing circumstances in which he was placed. He threw his arms about in a most singular manner, and his legs seemed to sympathise with his arms, for they were kept in constant motion. At length, he got up and took his usual draught, and returning to his chair closed his eyes. The strong drink he had taken did not tend to mend matters, for his brain had become none of the clearest : and now blinded by passion, he determined to act according to its present dictates. It would be the most egregious piece of folly, if he abandoned the plans which had cost him so much pain, anxiety, and trouble; besides, his mad passion for Mabel positively increased rather than diminished, under all his torments, supernatural and earthly, and would not allow him to give her up, despite the rash promise he had more than once made through fear; imbibing another draught from the flask, he called himself a poor silly fool, an egregious ass, for ever having given a moment's credence to apparitions, which at that moment, he pronounced to be mere mental delusions and nothing more. He determined to act more boldly and with greater decision, and at once, that very day to declare his love, and urge Mabel to become his before Jenkins had time to try his powers of persuasion. Little did Brewster imagine all that had occurred, and still less did he know or suspect the inclination of the widow's heart.

Having made up his mind, Brewster determined not to leave his house till night, for from what Thomas had said, his condition was known among his neighbours, and he felt no inclination to become an object of curiosity, therefore, despising for the moment, nocturnal apparitions, he determined to leave home, when darkness would shroud him from prying eyes, and learn his doom from Mabel's lips. If it should be favorable so much the better; but if his love should be rejected, he would still persevere; and by a system of persecution and perseverance he felt certain he should gain his object; for persecution and perseverance would win any woman. As to gaining Mabel's love, he gave himself no concern on that head, all he cared was to make her his wife.

CHAPTER V.

Nothing could be more unfortunate than the time the hag-ridden Doctor had chosen to make his declaration of love to the young widow.

Late as it was when Willie Sawyer had retired to rest, he arose early the following morning, and having satisfied the inner man with a substantial breakfast, he went, without delay to Mrs. Silverton's house, and, as was to be expected, recounted to her, in his most ludicrous style the chase after Brewster the night befo re.

"Oh! my dear Mabel, you should have witnessed the glorious hunt, I and my beagles had after your devoted lover!" Willie began, by way of preface to his narrative. "'Blue Skin' ran as no other animal ever ran before; his right leg beat the left, and then his left leg distanced his right, whilst his lanky arms kept pace with his legs—oh! it was a glorious chase. Tally ho! Tally ho! sang Sawyer:—

> "The moon was bright,
> The street it was light
> As we went in full chase,
> And ran down th' coward base!"
>
> Tally ho! Tally ho!"

"Well, coz," continued Willie; "on he sped, till my beagles came up with him, and then the frightened beast stood at bay till I arrived, considerably out of breath; he looked as wild as a hyena, and spurted forth the most egregious nonsense. I attempted to raise him, for he must needs faint, and we carried him back

to his house, when having dismissed my
fellow-hunters, I helped his crabbed servant
to convey him to bed. The suet-visaged
servitor told me that his master nightly
indulged in strong drinks, and in consequence
makes most awful rows, but never before indulged in such a one as that I witnessed."

" Poor man ! "—began Mabel.

" Poor beast ! " interrupted her cousin.
" His name's up, coz, so I've done with him.
Don't give him that tender heart of yours
there's a darling—don't give him your hand,
duckey—don't—"

" Oh ! Willie," interrupted Mabel, laughing
at the grimaces with which her cousin accom-
panied his entreaties, " how can you be so silly
—you need not fear—I am not going to give
Doctor Brewster either my heart, or my hand.
But," she continued more gravely, " I am
truly sorrow to hear what you have told me.

Poor man, he has been very kind to me, and I owe him much."

"I dare say you do," replied Willie, "but if ever I saw a crazy man in my life, he is one. So have your eyes and all your wits about you, Mabel, and get rid of him as quickly and quietly as you can. You would find it no joke to be shut up cheek by jowl, with a mad dog or a mad Doctor. Shake off the wily hypocrite, my darling. As sure as pigs are not pigeons, he'll try and frighten you into marrying him—so keep both eyes open, but shut both your ears to the insinuating words of the Adonis!"

"Nonsense Willie!" responded Mabel, but she could not prevent the remembrance of Brewster's looks and last words, and a cloud passed over her face.

"A penny for your thoughts," cried Sawyer, laughing, and looking slily into her face. "You look scared. I'll venture my head, the

snake has whispered something very sweet to
you, that is, if it be possible to extract sugar
from crab-apples—come, coz, what did he
say? "

"What should he say?"

" 'I love you, sweetest Mabel!" and Sawyer
dropped on his knees mimicking Brewster's voice
and manner, so well that in spite of his face
and form, he seemed present to his cousin.
'I love you better than man ever loved
woman—I adore you, and wish to make you
my wife, and I will cherish you till death
parts us!' "

"Willie, get up and don't be acting such
mad pranks" entreated Mabel. "I wish you
would be less wild."

"Well, my dear cousin," Willie said, rising
and taking both her hands in his, his look and
manner changing instantly, from buffoonery
to gravity. "I will be less wild—and help
you in your hour of need. You are alone and

unprotected. In spite of my follies, I can be
serious, and you may repose the utmost confidence in me. I can keep sacred your secrets,
and I can aid you with advice, when I lay
aside my vagaries."

He took a seat by his cousin's side, and no
man could be farther from anything approaching fun than he was at that moment.

"Now, Mabel, tell me what has passed,
between you and Brewster, so that I may know
how to act and what to do on your behalf.
You may safely rely on my prudence. It's a
strange word for such a rattle-brain as Willie
Sawyer, to apply to himself—but I *can* and
I *will* be prudent, cousin."

Mabel was naturally confiding; it was
neither in her age, sex nor nature to be otherwise : and Sawyer's manner was so affectionate
and so encouraging, and she felt such a
weight of nervous dread and loneliness
creeping back over her, which she longed to

shake off, that, with many sighs, she told Willie all that had passed since her husband's death.

Sawyer listened with the greatest attention to the recital, without interrupting her, and when she had finished, he snapped his fingers in the air, and made sundry knittings of his brow, and then looked at her and smiled as he remarked :—

" My dear cousin : I can plainly see through the man's schemes. That the miserable imp of malignity loves you, I do not doubt. Marry him ? why rather than you should commit such an egregious piece of folly, I'd positively wring your little white neck, with my own hands."

" Dear Willie please do not be so very violent."

" Well ! I will be gentle as a lamb," he said with a smile : and then after a minute's reflection he continued. "I would advise you to leave London. The spring is advancing, your country house will be getting a pleasant residence. I would also recommend that you remain away during the remainder of your year of widow-hood. I will take a lodging in the village, so that you will have a protector near you in case of emergency. Jenkins shall often come to see us, and we will spend a merry time together. Your daughter-in-law will be glad to go with you, for she says she hates London, and so in truth does she most things. But Mabel, say not a word of your plan, to that wretch Brewster."

Mabel blushed when Willie spoke of Doctor Jenkins. He observed it, and after waiting for her reply, which came not, he continued :—

"Think over what I have said. The sooner you go the better."

Mabel still remained silent.

"Jenkins," he began again, with a laugh, "Jenkins has done nothing but talk of you ever since he was here : that is when he *does* talk. Then he goes into a silent fit, and stares at nothing, unless it be that his imagination is portraying the features of Mabel Silverton ; then he smiles such a smile, I only wish you could see it, and rubs his hands with such evident pleasure—and then he breaks forth into such a burst of merriment all about nothing, just as if he had an inward bon-fire : then again he becomes dumb for a time, and only answers 'Yes,' or 'No,' like a charity child ; or like M. or N. in the catechism, '*as may be*' all of a sudden he begins to talk of you, and nothing leading to it, and so—and so—and so, Mabel, my darling, it's no use mincing the matter and pretending not to see the sun on a fine summer's day—it's as sure as that your delicate little hand is not an elephant's tusk, ———"

Here Willie cast a meaning smile upon his cousin. She knew what he was going to say, and her heart beat violently. She purposely let fall her handkerchief, and stooped to pick it up, but he was too quick for her, he darted upon it, and seizing her wrist held her fast, and putting his other hand under her chin, made her hold up her head, and continued :—

"Jenkins is madly in love with you, mistress Silverton!" then throwing the handkerchief over her head and face went on :—

"There's a veil to hide your blushes. Oh! by Jupiter, the veil looks as if it had a pink lining; never mind, my darling, but just listen."

Mabel pulled the veil from her head, but she could not refrain from laughing and reproving her cousin.

"Well," Willie said, "I see I'm in disgrace, so I'll just make myself scarce; but first listen to my last dying speech! You can't do a

better or a wiser thing, than to fall desperately
in love with Peter.   Marry as soon as you can,
and give him the right to protect you from
that wretch Brewster, whose lies about Peter
are without the slightest foundation, for there
is not under heaven a more generous open
hearted fellow.   The other ugly brute wanted
you for himself. By Jove ! what a brilliant idea
—only fancy a little white dove, nestling with
an evil-eyed carrion crow !   Good bye, Mabel.
Dream of Peter Jenkins, and in your prayers
night and morning, don't forget your loving
cousin," and much to the surprise of Mabel,
he jumped over one of the chairs, and left the
room.

After the conversation just related, it will
readily be understood that Mabel was in no
mood to give Doctor Brewster or his tender
avowals a very cordial reception.   On the
contrary, the mere thought of his calling
troubled her so, that she trembled and her

mind revolted—and she was obliged to call to
her aid, the many kindnesses he had done her
in past days, and to get up a sort of pity for
his present unhappy condition, before her
gentle mind could be satisfied with it's
feelings, and then to dismiss him, as well as
she was able, from her thoughts. Every step she
heard on the stairs alarmed her, she was so
fearful of a visit from him, and she rejoiced as
the day closed, that he had not made his
appearance.

She was more than pleased, she was delighted with all that her cousin had said of
Jenkins, and she began to realise what it was
to be alone with only herself to trust to. The
thought chilled her young heart, and she forthwith, even then, clung to the image of her lover,
and felt a sense of security even in thinking
of him; to confess the truth, the young widow
solaced her anxiety by remembering his words,
tones and looks, trying to gather from them if

Sawyer's assertions were true, or only his wild way of jesting. Sometimes she felt assured that Jenkins still loved her, and the idea caused a feeling of safety and rest; then she doubted and sighed; she again and again brought to her recollection the conversation in the lane, his memorable confession; and the pressure of his hand—and his pleasurable looks as he parted from her the day before. All re-assured her, and so without any amount of trouble or self-reproach, she was carrying out Willie Sawyer's advice, and every minute was sinking deeper and deeper into the abyss of love.

The evening was rapidly passing away, the early supper had terminated, and Mabel's unamiable daughter-in-law had gone to her own apartment, leaving the widow to follow the bent of her inclinations in any way that she might chose. She took up a book, but did not attempt to read, her thoughts were too busily employed, but Brewster was in no way connected with these thoughts—Peter Jenkins entirely and exclusively engrossed them. She was, however, interrupted by the old man servant whose footsteps sounded on the stairs—he opened the door, and after announcing the devoted Brewster retired.

Mrs. Silverton laid down her book and rose to receive him, and if her heart beat at his first entry it redoubled its throbs as he approached nearer to her. Instead of his usual quiet, steady step, and downcast eyes, he advanced with a quick pace, almost approaching a run, and staring at her with fiery looks, whilst his small eyes gleamed in their blood-shot whites like those of some savage animal. On his cheeks a scarlet spot was not only visible but vied with the blush on his nose. He had omitted to remove his hat which stuck at the back of his head, giving him an almost idiotic appearance; his shirt collar was much tumbled, and what was worst of all his chin was unshaven, giving him a positively dirty appearance.

He took Mabel by both hands and placed her somewhat roughly in a chair, his hat dropping on the floor; then he took a seat close beside her.

Mrs. Silverton's cheek paled, she not only felt some alarm lest his violence should become more demonstrative, but she was at once made acquainted with the fact that Doctor Brewster had been fortifying himself with ardent spirits, for the odour floated around her. She trembled from head to foot and shrunk from the look of sensuous admiration, with which Brewster was silently indulging himself. It was not one of those usually studied, timid, half-averted looks scarcely observable and more felt than seen, but an unmistakable stare, from one who considered he had a right to exercise that right to the full bent of his inclination.

The alarmed Mrs. Silverton's first impulse was to rise and run from the room, but her knees shook and she could scarcely breathe. She, however, ventured to raise her eyes, and look upon his face, but the horrible smile, or rather grin which was enthroned there, struck her with a feeling of awe, that chained her speechless to the spot.

For some time neither seemed disposed to speak, Brewster continuing to stare and Mabel to tremble. At length he threw one of his lanky arms over the back of her chair, and stooping forward, he took possession of her cold, trembling and unresisting hand.

" How very cold your hand is " he said at length. Mabel endeavoured to release it, but he held it fast in his skeleton claw which was hot and feverish.

Mabel did not see his triumphant look, but

she heard him chuckle, and then speak, not in his usual demure, winning way, but in a hoarse harsh tone of voice: and to her horror and dismay he pressed her hand, which he held in an iron grasp, close to his breast.

"You know, Mabel, that I have long felt the greatest interest in your welfare," he said, "but although you know this, there is one thing which you have yet to learn, and that is my love for you."

Brewster felt the effort Mabel was making to free her little hand, but he knew it was safe in his keeping and he went on:

"It is no use my making further attempts to hide it from you. It is burning into my very heart, day and night. I know no rest, for your image is always before me. I can think of you and you only. Oh, dearest Mabel, I want you to become my wife at once —I wish to save you from that heartless, vain, riotous, living Jenkins, who is drawing his nets tighter and tighter around you, and compassing you with snares, so that he may obtain possession of your money; for yourself he cares not. I love you! I adore you! with a love passing all things. I cannot and I will not live without you."

Mabel felt the arm that had rested on the back of her chair passed round her small waist. A shudder went through her whole frame, chill and cold. Se tried to move—to speak, but she could do neither one nor the other. She turned her head away from him, and he went on:

"Mabel, my dearest Mabel, will you be mine—will you be my wife? I have loved you for years in silence;—I have envied your husband his happiness—I have waited year after year, month after month, and day after day meekly and patiently till you should be free—Will you now be my wife?"

This last sentence was uttered tremulously

but hoarsely. Mabel turned towards him, but could not speak, and he taking her silence and agitation for an avowal of love and an acceptance of his suit, pressed his burning lips on her white forehead. In this blissful state of ignorance Brewster considerably relaxed the grip of her hand, and the moment she felt thus released, she started from him as though a snake had coiled its shining body around her; and bursting into tears, she leaned for support on the high back of a chair.

Brewster also started up and said tenderly endeavouring to remove her hands from her face :—

" Do not weep, my dearest Mabel, I can easily understand your surprise !—your joy— and would save you the pain of uttering your consent in words; darling, give me one fond kiss. It shall be the seal of your consent to my wishes, and the bond of our future happiness ! "

The widow checked her sobs, and with a violent effort composed herself; and after a brief pause, said : —

"Doctor Brewster, do not deceive yourself, I can never be your wife!"

Anger and surprise took possession of the Doctor's bosom.

"Never!" he cried in the voice of a demon, and then mastering his passion, he said, in as soft a tone as he could : "Mabel, you will be the death of me, if you speak thus. I am dying for you already. Say only that you love me. I know—I am sure you do. Let no false shame prevent your telling me so. Say only, 'I love you!' say dearest—— "

"I have already spoken, Doctor Brewster, and I mean what I have said," replied Mabel, in a feeble voice, but with considerable firmness, and making an effort, she moved towards the door. Brewster's passion got the better of his judgment. He rushed after her, and seizing her in his arms held her with all his strength.

"You shall be mine" he cried, his eyes gleaming on her with mingled love and rage. "you shall swear that you will be my wife. I will not let go my hold till you have solemnly pledged yourself that you will be mine. As for your love, I care not for it. You may hate and detest me, but, with hate or love, you shall be my wife!"

Mabel felt that all her efforts to free herself from his grasp would be vain, and she nearly fainted with horror.

All that Willie Sawyer had told her of the Doctor's madness, now came vividly to her mind, and his deeds confirmed that all he had heard was true. She knew that she was alone and unprotected in the hands of a violent maniac.

Brewster set his teeth and grinned demoniacally, and shaking her in a most savage manner said:

"Speak — swear! Fool! say you will be mine—I love you!"

Mabel's terror became fearful. She could not utter a word, and Brewster, holding her at arm's length, shook her, ground his teeth, and stared at her like a triumphant demon.

All in a moment his grasp relaxed and he let go his hold; he became, in an instant, pale as death, all colour retreating from his sallow countenance, his teeth chattered and he trembled more violently than the weak woman he had been persecuting. His eyes became suddenly fixed on a point behind her. There stood the misty form of poor old Silverton. The stern, cold eyes and frowning brow were commanding and firm, and he pointed towards the door, with his bleeding out-stretched arm. Brewster stood horrified and shrunk within himself. A peal of laughter sounded close beside him. The squalid old hag seized his arm, and mocking at him patted his cheek with her long, shrivelled, bony fingers, and led him, without his making the slightest resistance, but shaking in every limb, from the house.

The widow dropt on her knees, and hiding her eyes on a chair wept till exhaustion ended her paroxysm. She was now quite convinced that Doctor Brewster's mind was gone. His extraordinary conduct and his sudden change from rage and passion to mute trembling fear and shrinking dread, his departure and silence, wild horrified looks and deadly hue, what were they? she asked herself. Unmistakable signs of madness. Her heart sickened and her frame shook past control, when she reflected that she had been in the grip of such a man alone, and with no one near to render her the slightest assistance.

CHAPTER VI.

When Willie Sawyer paid his daily visit to his cousin the morning following Doctor Brewster's frantic outbreak, it may be well imagined that he did not find her in her usual spirits.

She had passed an almost sleepless night, and when she had closed her eyes in sleep, it was only to dream the most harrowing dreams in which Doctor Brewster's frantic outbreaks held a conspicuous place; and when she awoke the whole scene of the previous evening appeared a turbulent, horrible, unconnected vision.

What to do Mabel knew not. The idea of ever again seeing Brewster she could not dwell upon, so completely and effectually had he terrified her; of his madness she had no longer the slightest doubt, and she could not help heaving a sigh of concern at his hapless condition. Then arose in her mind the question—how was she to be protected from him? She thought of her cousin; but the idea was immediately dismissed. He could not reside under the same roof with her. She thought of Peter Jenkins, and she gave a deeper sigh, but her sigh was of a very different character to that she had given to Brewster, the latter was lighter than the former, this was deep drawn and tremulous, and it was followed by a short reverie devoted to the object of the deep-sigh aforesaid, and extremely favorable to the latter's views and plans.

Her head ached painfully, but still she continued to think over the subject, of to whom she should appeal for succour in her hour of trial. At length she remembered an only brother of her late husband's, an old man, who was living a very retired life in Cornwall. This brother was a married man, and Mabel had never seen his wife, but Nicholas Silverton was tolerably well known to her, and she knew that he was a kind-hearted, straight-forward man; she was certain he would take her to his home.

This idea, of Nicholas Silverton becoming her protector, gave great joy to her heart, but, alas! it was a fleeting joy, for a few minutes after she recollected that there had been a coolness between the two brothers, in conse-quence of their religious opinions, her husband being a strict dissenter, and Nicholas Silverton a high churchman. Then she turned to reflect again on her lonely condition, and, as might be expected, Peter Jenkins, again took possession of her thoughts, and she began to

consider whether it would be more desirable
to seek safety at a distance from him, or
danger near him. The latter notion gave her
the most pleasure : and she commenced a
series of difficulties about her brother-in-law
and his wife, the latter might not be disposed to
receive her, and the former might not wish a
dissenter to be a companion to his children, at
this point of her cogitations, the voice of
Sawyer was heard :—

" All ready for a start," cried Willie, coming
into the room in his usual merry way. " My
dear cousin, Peter and I have arranged everything for you. We have agreed to be your
body guard : and the sooner you get away
from this dull place, the better, I can tell
you ! "

" Why, Willie ? "

" Why, my pretty innocence. Peter and I
have been to look at the wild beast, and pronounce it dangerous ! The animal foams at

the mouth, and a very dirty mouth it is—
swearing and cursing in a manner that quite
shocked my sensitive nerves."

" What, Doctor Brewster? you surely do not
mean Doctor Brewster."

" I do though. He is as fierce as a tiger-
cat. His man, Thomas, can't manage him;
so he sent for Jenkins, and I went to look on.
The poor wretch is not mad enough to warrant strong measures being adopted; but
Thomas says he didn't to go to bed, but was
hullabalooing all night. When Peter entered
his room, the mad beast flew at him like a
tiger. I seized and held him, till Peter paci-
fied him a little. So you see, Mabel, it
will be wise if you start to-night."

Mabel made no objection—and to tell the
truth she was quite as willing and ready to
go as Willie could wish. She gave her cousin
an account of her dreadful interview with
Brewster the previous evening, Sawyer turned

up his eyes, and whistled a long note, by way
of symphony when his cousin's tale came to an
end, pronouncing or rather denouncing Brewster, in terms by no means flattering, and then
turning to Mabel he said :—

"No wonder, sweet coz, you are looking so
white!"

"My head aches dreadfully, Iv'e had
scarcely any sleep."

"And you are feverish," he replied, affec
tionately taking her hand, and folding her
little white fingers in his broad, brown palms.
"You require a Doctor."

"Not just now, Willie," she said, hurriedly ;
and then she told him her idea about visiting
her brother-in-law.

"Well, I will think that over. I can't
decide the point at once," and Sawyer took
his leave determining to consult his friend Peter
ere he decided. He found Jenkins pacing his
room to and fro with his hands clasped behind

him, he was evidently not in good spirits, for he
was not humming a love ditty, and thinking of
the widow Silverton!—No—of Doctor Brewster, and what was to be his probable end.

"Halt!" cried Sawyer catching his friend's
arm, "You are wanted. I've got a new
patient for you—She's very bad, and will
require all your skill to cure her—come along
my lad."

And Sawyer put Jenkins' hat upon his
head the wrong side before, and literally
dragged him out of the house.

"Who is this new patient?" asked Jenkins
righting his hat.

"I am in too much hurry to be able to
speak," said Sawyer, "but if you will step
out a bit you'll soon see."

This was all the information Peter could
elicit, but he soon saw by the route his guide
took, that it was to Lime Street he was being
conducted.

"What is the matter with her?" asked Jenkins anxiously.

"How can I tell—I'm no Doctor!"

"Sawyer, you are a provoking devil!" said Peter.

"Am I?"

"Yes."

"Ingrate!" said Willie, "I have—well, never mind—come along."

They arrived at the widow's residence, and reached her presence. Sawyer placed a chair next to Mabel's, and in the most graceful manner intimated to Jenkins, that he should instal himself in it; then informing them that he must leave for a short time, till the consultation was over, he quitted the room.

Jenkins looked at Mabel, and Mabel turned away her head. Jenkins took her hand and applied his fingers to her pulse, and an extraordinary pulse beat beneath them, whilst his throbbed in a manner tenfold more extraordinary. After clearing his voice, he enquired, with his utmost courtesy, and a sufficient degree of tenderness, after her health, just by way of introduction, for he was perfectly aware of the entire cause of her malady.

Being answered, and having again spoken and having been again answered, he moved his chair to a respectful distance, seeing that Sawyer had placed it very near to Mabel's, nearer than etiquette might warrant. After accomplishing this change he said :—

"I think you require change of air, Mrs. Silverton, and the sooner you get into the country the better."

"So my cousin says, Doctor Jenkins. He wished me to depart this evening."

Here Mabel paused for a moment, and then continued :—

"I should wish it too; yet I do not

feel as if I were fit for a journey—but—I—
that is—Willie—" and she paused again,
whereupon Peter, drawing his chair a little
nearer, said with much tenderness.

"Mrs. Silverton, there is no need for such
haste. Remain till the morning and fear not.
I will take care that you receive neither insult
nor alarm. Your cousin has told me what
has befallen you, and what you have suffered
—I burn with anger when I think of it."

Mabel thanked him; when she looked on his
handsome face, all the calumnies Brewster
had invented were scattered to the winds, and
dismissed from her mind, with a mingling of
contempt and pity, as the malicious invention
of a disordered brain.

There was silence for some few minutes,
each occupied with his or her own train of
thought. Mabel looked through the window
as if interested by something at a distance.

Jenkins looked at his boots, then at Mabel, and being so engaged when she turned to speak to him, he quietly transferred his looks elsewhere, taking the privilege of one addressed to turn them on her again.

"I shall scarcely feel secure so near London," she said. "Has my cousin told you that I had proposed to myself to go to my brother-in-law, in Cornwall?"

Sawyer had made no mention of it, and the information gave Jenkins no pleasure.

"No, he said nothing to me on the subject," he replied, his hopes sinking down to freezing point. He had flattered himself that he was making a favorable impression on the widow, but now he began mentally to call himself an idiot, for entertaining such an idea. Could she meditate a journey so long and difficult, with such slight communication with the capital—could she meditate this species of exile from London and care for him.

Mabel saw the expression of disappointment cloud his face : her heart throbbed, and she rejoiced, and grieved at the same time. There was another pause, Mabel again looking through the window, and Peter at his boots, but his heart was in a tumult. He more than half determined to declare his love for her at once—then he felt inclined to leave her for ever, calling himself a fool for having thrown away so much time on love. He knit his brows, and it was well that Mabel was still gazing through the window, or she might have fancied by the fierce flashing of his eyes, that the spirit of Brewster had been transferred to the body of Jenkins, and was at her side.

He turned his head sharply round, to pronounce his farewell, but Mabel looked so quiet, so meek, so sorrowful, as to cause all his momentary anger to vanish. He could not, however, get up his hopes again in an instant, but instead of his burning anger he felt a quiet sorrow.

"I have not determined," Mabel said, "upon going to my brother-in-law's, for the distance is very great. Besides I have some fears about my reception."

Mabel felt that it would be difficult to leave Peter, though she did not exactly acknowledge as much to herself: nor did she understand that the longer she remained near him, the less able she would be to leave, so Peter, after this little speech of her's, began to hope she might not go at all.

"I think," he began, "you would be perfectly safe and free from annoyance in your own country house; but yet, if you do not feel that you would be secure there, whatever I may desire, I would not wish you to remain in town."

Another pause took place, and another look through the window by Mabel, and another

survey of the boots by Jenkins. At length
the latter prepared to speak, but what he meant
to say, or what would have resulted from his
words, I know not, for at the moment Sawyer
entered the room and prevented his friend
Peter making public, what he had been on the
very verge of declaring.

"Well, most wise and sapient Doctor, is
your patient to live or die?"

"To live, I trust, to enjoy many years of
happiness," said Peter rising.

"Are we to march to-night? and undertake the safe conduct of this distressed
damsel from the hobgoblin who adores her!"

"I have advised Mrs. Silverton not to start
till to-morrow. I think a night's rest will be
desirable; and if on the morrow she will
permit me to ride beside her, in company with
you, I shall be most delighted to do so."

Mabel thanked Jenkins and consented.

"But suppose the goblin puts in an appearance again to-night," asked Sawyer "with his loving ways, honied words and most pleasant smiles!"

Mabel shivered and Jenkins replied.

"Leave the goblin, as you call him, to me. I will engage that he shall molest no one to-night."

They left Mabel to repose, and Billy had the gratification of conveying a very delectable and soothing mixture to her, and thereby passing a whole hour with his *inamorata* Susan, to whom he had just addressed the following words :—

"I love you, and you do love I, don't we?" when in stalked Mrs. Silverton's step-daughter, putting a stop to all the titterings, and laughings, and small talk, which they had been indulging in to make time pass pleasantly. No sooner, however, had this pleasant apparition made her appearance, than away went the smiles, and the before happy couple were reduced to looks of blank solemnity, the faint lines around their mouths, and the moisture of their eyes, being the only tokens chased merriment left behind.

" Shame—shame—shame ! " began the amiable lady, making each ' shame ' longer, louder and deeper than the preceding. " Why do I hear this unseemly noise and merriment, oh ! man ! oh ! maid ! Fie ! fie upon you both. Leave this place man. Get thee gone. And you, unholy damsel, let me never catch you in such wicked company again. Man, depart instantly, and you girl take your sewing."

Susan took her work without daring to cast a single glance upon the astonished Billy, who was compelled to leave the room : the amiable spinster literally driving him before her. She then sought her step-mother, and learning her intended departure, with her usual pleasant

manner, and most amiable tone of voice,
said ;—

"You can do just as you please, Mrs.
Silverton, but I shall remain here. I cannot
consent to associate with the wild, rakish men
that have of late visited you, causing blushes to
rise to my cheeks; and never allowing me to
walk about the house, without the fear of one or
other rushing from every corner to kiss me.
Here I will stay. Not content with that most
wicked, and most wilful of men, your cousin
Sawyer, you must need bring into your house,
the Doctor of all the spendthrift lords and
ladies—vile ungodly men and women, one and
all. Not a minute since I caught the Doctor's
servant, laughing and jesting, and I verily
believe making love to your maid-servant—I
drove him from the house, as I would have
driven a crow from a corn-field. No, no, Mrs.
Silverton, I will not have my ears offended or
my feelings irritated by such evil-minded men,

as have lately forced their way into my presence. I will stay here," and away went the right-minded lady to her room, and her own meditations.

Doctor Jenkins, ere day-light fled and the evening had set in, wended his way to Doctor Brewster's, whom he found sitting alone in a very melancholy state of mind, and considerably exhausted. The fearful excitement he had undergone the previous night was no longer visible. His spirits had left him, and he sat moping and dejected, thinking over his failing projects, and conjuring up spectres and visions, and the evil deeds he had done in days bygone, trembling for the future, but with his intense and ardent love for Mabel as strong as ever.

"I will torment and persecute her," he soliloquised: "she shall be mine—she shall marry first, and love will follow—yes, yes! mine she shall be. That bleeding shall not be thrown away. Bleeding! ah! ah! ah! Bleeding! how it spurted out and trickled on the basin. How she fixed her lovely eyes on mine. How she pressed my hands. How she trembled! Let a thousand spectres stand before us, she shall be my wife! She may reject my proposals a thousand times but I will persevere!"

This was all very magnanimous, but Brewster trembled and felt ill, and Jenkins saw that he was so—Brewster sulkily stretched out his arm for Jenkins to feel his pulse, and answered moodily the questions put to him.

"You must keep yourself as quiet as possible."

"Ah!" replied Brewster.

"If your man will get me what I want I will make up a mixture for you to take, and the sooner you get to bed the better. I will not ail seeing you the first thing in the morning."

"Thomas!" shouted Brewster, and the

surly servant made his appearance, and being told to shew Doctor Jenkins into a dingy back room, they left the patient; and Peter taking down from the shelves several dirty, dusky-looking bottles, proceeded to make the mixture he required. During the process, Thomas said :—

" He's as touchy as a young colt!—He's as peevish as a spoilt child !—He's as crazy as a man well can be!"

Jenkins made no remark, and Thomas finding that he was not inclined to speak, followed his example and said no more.

Having completed the mixture, Jenkins took it to his patient in a glass that had not come in contact with clean water for a considerable time.

" Here, Brewster, take this off at once," said Jenkins.

Without a word Brewster emptied the glass of its contents.

" You may go," he said.

Jenkins obeyed the polite dismissal, and withdrew.

In a very short time after Jenkins had left the house, Brewster became very drowsy and very calm, and went to bed, and in a few minutes his senses were enveloped in a quiet stupor.

Thomas had an undisturbed night, such as he had not known for weeks, and felt almost grateful to Doctor Jenkins ; that is as far as he was capable of being grateful, for gratitude was not one of his besetting sins.

Jenkins, in his gallant anxiety for Mabel, had administered an opiate to Brewster, strong enough to bind him over to keep the peace for that one night at all events.

CHAPTER VII.

After Sawyer and Doctor Jenkins had taken their leave of Mabel, she felt exceedingly low aud out of spirits in her country house. She had been very happy during the drive, for Jenkins and Sawyer had ridden one on each side of her coach, that is when the roads were wide enough to admit of such escort. Time had sped pleasantly with the three.

Jenkins, whose hopes, which after divers combats and doubts, during which his friend Willie had not found him very agreeable, were again in the ascendant, and his conversation on the journey was marked by lively sallies and pleasant witticisms. As they rode through the ever-memorable lane, he squeezed his horse perilously between the hedge and the coach wheels, and putting his head in at the window, after a minute withdrew it and fell into the rear looking remarkably happy and smiling. Mabel appeared equally happy and smiling, whilst a blush suffused her countenance, Jenkins probably having recalled some bygone event to her memory.

They left her, and she was alone in the parlour where Jenkins had spent so many happy hours the first day of their acquaintance. It was a cold spring evening in the beginning of April, but the dry cutting March wind still prevailed, the sheep and lambs bleating under shelter of the hedge-rows. The sky was very clear and pale, and the sinking sun, not low enough to be red, looked as though the chill

wind had given him cold. The rooks were
loudly cawing and returning to the trees, the
branches of which, though leafless, looking
owing to their buds, thicker and more shadowy
than they had done during the winter. The
wind rushed bleak and cold round the old house,
roared down the chimney and whistled through
the key hole. The house dog, a splendid
fellow, which had been a great favorite with
poor Mr. Silverton, was trotting about rattling
his collar and reminding Mabel of past times,
when she so often saw him running by his
master's side, as fresh and healthy he returned
from his evening walk—Where was that master
now? In his grave, laid low by a villanous
Doctor. Mabel wept, as every thing around
her served to recall her husband and his great
kindness to her memory.

Immediately opposite to her hung his portrait in a plain oak frame, and close beside was
her own, painted when she was a child, a little

fair stiff creature dressed in blue velvet. This portrait had been prized most highly by her late husband. His gun hung over the mantel-piece —and his easy chair and writing desk stood in their usual places. On the table cover was a large ink spot and Mabel sighed as she remembered the day on which her husband, writing in haste, had made it—his laugh and merry humour at his awkwardness still rung in her ears. These and a hundred other such memories placed him as it were beside her, and she felt less helplessly miserable as she looked at the cheerful, open, amiable expression of the face which seemed to smile tenderly on her from his portrait.

It appeared almost impossible that sturdy looking man should indeed be dead. Mabel wept for her husband, and she loved Peter Jenkins. The two loves were not incompatible. As her tear moistened eyes looked sadly on the picture of the dead, the living image of Jenkins was in her heart and his words and tender voice in her ears.

Her late husband's old serving man placed supper before her, and, observing her tears, lingered near and tried to console her in his simple way; talked to her of his lost master, lamented over him, and shook his head; then advised her to keep a strong heart and take comfort, and even ventured to shake her hand with his hard and trembling fingers, and then left her to cogitate over her past and present misery and happiness.

She took up a pondrous bible from which her late husband had been in the habit of reading morning and evening, and commenced at the portion he had usually read, and perused the passages he had marked. They all tended to calm and soothe her mind. They were the reflex of his own spirit, placid, amiable, cheerful, firm, compassionate and contented. There were also many marginal notes written by his

own hand.   Mabel passed the whole evening
reading the bible with her husband's annota-
tions, and the occupation brought peace.

"Oh! how much better he is out of the
world of trial and sin," she thought; then she
reflected over all the incidents of the good
old man's last days, and especially remembered
her horror at finding him dead by her side.
She hid her eyes in her hands and shuddered.
The report of Brewster's ravings came like a
flash of lightning to her mind and in her
goodness she would have excused what she
thought might be an error, caused by his
unhappy state of mind.   The idea was a
torment to her when she reflected, but for
that error her husband might still have been
alive: it banished peace and sleep : grief and
terror no longer existed, that one idea absorbed
her entirely.   She thought, and thought truly,
but for Brewster her husband might still have

been alive and in health. She retired to rest but not to sleep.

The next day Mrs. Silverton waited anxiously for a visit from Jenkins, to whom she imparted all her grief and all her fears respecting Brewster's treatment of her husband. Peter questioned her as to every particular of Mr. Silverton's illness, and the treatment he had received.

Mabel did not observe the expression of anger that flitted over his countenance at the close of her history. Jenkins at once saw how the case stood, saw that Brewster had murdered the poor old gentleman; and it was with the greatest difficulty that he mastered his feelings of rage and emotion. He, however, kept his secret to himself and soothed Mabel's alarm and anxiety by telling her that everything had been done for the best; and he saw with delight the cloud that overshadowed her pass away. He perfectly understood that Mr.

Silverton's blood had flowed to make Mabel Brewster's, and owned that his present state of mental agony was a just punishment for his iniquities. He had now a sure clue to his disordered intellect, and in his kindness of heart, pity for his sin and degradation mingled with his contempt and anger.

Jenkins' contempt was farther strengthened by words that dropped from Brewster's own lips. That unhappy, sinful man was prevented carrying out his plan of persecuting Mabel, by a fierce raging fever, during which he raved wildly of the dark secrets of his diabolical soul, announcing horrid deeds into the ears of Jenkins and Thomas, the only two persons who were permitted to approach him. These ravings revealed acts of diabolical iniquity he had practised. He told how men, enfeebled by sickness, had their minds worked upon to discard all family ties and make their fortunes his. There were deeds of cruelty and wrong,

done in secret, now disclosed with restless
tossing in his bed or in low moaning. A cold
shiver ran through his frame as he upbraided
himself from having consigned one to starva-
tion and death in some horrible place, a beautiful woman carried off by stealth from husband
and home, there to perish; one he had loved
in spite of all her hate. At length came the
terror of his last infamous exploit and the way
in which it was accomplished.

Dr. Jenkins stood by Brewster's bed, who
raved and rolled his gleaming eyes, grasped
the bed-clothes, and literally howled in terror,
or cowered beneath the coverlet in trembling
dread. He called on Mabel in terms of the
utmost endearment; then reproached her with
ingratitude for refusing to become his wife,
he who had done so much to win her—then
he entreated for mercy as he fancied the spectral
Silverton looked sternly on him, and he cowered
still more as he fancied the haggard old woman

pulled the bed-clothes from his grasp, laughing loudly and grinning at him as she walked around and around his bed. He strove to throw himself from it and drive her from the room, and then it was that the united strength of Jenkins and the man-servant had to be exerted to force him back again. Thin and meagre as he was, his strength, in his delirium was such as almost to defy all their efforts.

Jenkins looked upon him with horror, but used every effort to save his miserable life. He could not bear to see a human being perish in the midst of blasphemy and unrepented crimes. His utmost attention and care were therefore devoted to him. Both day and night he was with him; and much as he loved Mabel, days were taken from her to be given to Brewster.

After a fortnight's ceaseless delirium the patient slept, and Jenkins sat dozing by his bed-side till he awoke, sensible. A terrible dread crept over him when he understood his situation. Jenkins drew back the bed-curtains and answered his feebly spoken questions. Death appeared at hand. A course of iniquity seemed drawing to a close. Life could only be saved by a miracle. Doctor Jenkins knew it well, and, doing as he would have wished to have been done by, he seriously told Brewster what he thought of his case, and urged him to prepare for death.

The sick man gazed vacantly for a minute and then by a sudden effort of strength got up on his knees. Jenkins expected that it was his intention to pray, and his heart gladdened, but his pleasure was of short duration.

" Die ! " shouted Brewster in an unearthly voice, " Die !—save me—save me from death, I cannot die—I *will* not die. Oh ! Jenkins, do not let me die. You have ever been my friend, save me now—pray save my life " and he folded his shaking hands as though about to pray, raised them above his head and stared anxiously, wildly, and imploringly upon Jenkins, who felt sickened and disgusted at his words and looks. Conscious that all his efforts would be of no avail to turn his thoughts into a right course, he took his arm and said :—

" Calm yourself, Brewster ; lie down, I am doing every thing I can devise for you. Compose your thoughts, and do not be so unmanly. I may yet be able, through God's mercy, to save you. But do not lose time, look on death and repent, lest you again become delirious, when repentance may be impossible—Shall I send for a minister of your own sect ? "

"Send for no one; it would kill me " cried Brewster, snatching his arm from Jenkins' hold and springing from his bed. He reeled to and fro both from weakness and giddiness, and falling at Jenkins' feet, clung to his knees as an imploring victim would cling to his murderer, and called upon him to save him.

"Oh! Jenkins, do not let me die! Save—save my life, or you will send me to everlasting torments!—Promise—swear that you will save me. Oh! I will not die— I *will* live—Do spare me—do save me from worse than death—from everlasting torment. You can save me if you like—Speak—pray speak—will you save me?"

Brewster's voice sounded sepulchral in the silence of night. His cadaverous countenance seen by the dim light of the lamp, and his agonised, clinging grasp, so full of despair and dread, told the intensity of his sufferings. Jenkins endeavoured to disengage himself and to raise the poor wretch from his kneeling posture.

"Brewster, I have already told you that I will do everything in my power to save you, but you must remember I am only, like yourself, a mortal man. Come, return to your bed, or you will be your own destroyer. Endeavour to calm yourself, or, as you well know, all my efforts will be fruitless. Lie down, or I will leave you to your fate at once, whatever it may be. What I say, I mean; so get back to your bed immediately."

Brewster tried to walk, but he was helpless as a child, and suffered himself to be placed in the bed. To calm his agitation was easier said than done; now that his conscience had full sway, and death stared him in the face, to be calm was impossible. As well might one try to lie quiet on a sheet of red-hot iron, as to live and face death with an evil conscience, alive to all its iniquities. He was fully aware of his sins and dreaded his end; and yet, strange to say, he did not loathe them. He still continued imploring for mercy—but he did not plead to his God,—he cried to mortal man to save him.

Jenkins watched the wretched man narrowly and eagerly, administered to him the remedies his body required, but his soul, he feared, was beyond cure. Still he cared for it, and rousing Thomas, who was soundly sleeping in the next room, sent him grumbling and swearing in quest of Brewster's spiritual adviser.

In less than half an hour the minister arrived, a meek and amiable looking old man, with face pale and grave, his hair nearly grey. In his countenance there did not appear a particle of selfishness, no traces of worldly feelings. He carried a small bible in his hand.

Jenkins rose to meet him, and without a word respectfully took his hand and led him to the bedside. He then told him that his patient stood in need of him, and in a whisper said that he had but little hopes of his recovery. Jenkins then retired to the next room leaving them alone, but remaining alert, fearful lest

Brewster in one of his paroxysms might roughly handle the gentle old man.

The minister drew a chair to the side of the bed, and in his feeble, aged voice began to speak of comfort to the sufferer, but every sentence added stab on stab to Brewster's soul. He listened as though spell bound. Each word gave him intense pain, and conjured terror upon terror. He tossed his head from side to side of the pillow, ground his teeth, and breathed hard, with closed eyes. The minister spoke soothingly to him, hoping to bring him to the point he wished, endeavouring to turn him, despite himself, to righteousness.

"Do you feel, my good friend, all I have said?" he mildly asked, laying his shrivelled fingers tenderly on the equally thin but burning hand, which lay trembling on the coverlet. Is there anything you would say—anything you would disclose to me?"

Brewster only groaned and the minister, still holding his hand, continued to speak to him words of comfort, as well as words of encouragement; for though Jenkins had told him Brewster needed repentance, he had not the slightest idea from what a miserable load of guilt he was suffering. After listening awhile the sick man suddenly opened his eyes, and starting up, seized the old man by the shoulders, and looking fiercely upon him said :—

"Can you save my life ? "

The minister shook like a child in his grasp, animal courage age had taken from him, but he lacked not moral courage, and he replied calmly :—

"I have nothing to do with the life of your body, my friend. Neither at such a moment as this should you regard it. Turn away your thoughts from earth to Heaven ! Look to your immortal soul I beseech you. Think only of what importance that is ! "

" Can you save my life ? " asked Brewster savagely, again shaking the poor old man with considerable violence.

" No, I cannot."

" Then get out of the house ! " and Brewster dashed him away and rolled himself in agony on his bed.

Jenkins who had heard Brewster's loud voice, rushed into the room, caught the old man in his arms and saved him from falling.

"I fear, Sir," said the Minister, " my words have had little effect, and yet I will not abandon him." Again he approached the bed, and Jenkins stood watchful by his side to shield him from harm. All efforts were in vain, Brewster heeded him not, but only cried for Jenkins to save him, and at length grew furious against the minister, who still maintained his post, nor withdrew till morning dawned, when Brewster was again raving in delirium, lost to all outward things, sensible only to the horrid visions that floated through his brain, and rehearsing all the crimes he had been guilty of.

The worthy minister shook Jenkins kindly by the hand, and sorrowfully departed, having been promised that he should be recalled should his services be required. Jenkins also left for awhile. Returning in a couple of hours, he found Brewster still in danger. Thomas, not expecting Jenkins' return so soon, having tied him down in his bed, raving and crying, was enjoying a good breakfast of his own providing in the kitchen.

Jenkins reproached him for his bad conduct to which he replied:

"Bless ye, sir, it makes no difference to he. How should he know? He never lets me have a bit of peace with my meals, so you see, it's my turn now."

Brewster's fever came to a crisis, and Jenkins awaited the turn with great anxiety. His life hung by a thread. What would be the result—would he live or die?

Brewster had an iron constitution and in spite of much that told against him, and which would have killed most men, he began slowly to recover, and the end of the month of May beheld him crawling from his room to taste the fresh air of heaven, at a farm house some miles from town, where he had been sent by Jenkins in an opposite direction to that in which Mabel was living, thus guarding her against any intrusion.

CHAPTER VIII.

During the time that Brewster had been tossing and raving on his sick bed, Mrs. Silverton had been enjoying tranquillity in her country retreat. Although Jenkins had spent much time in attendance upon his rival, he had paid frequent visits to Mabel, and he felt more than happy in the progress he had made towards gaining her affections: that their regard and love for each was mutual, was now beyond the possibility of a doubt. She no longer deemed it requisite to seek a retreat with her late husband's brother, nor did Willie Sawyer

deem it important that he should take up his
abode in the village as he had promised, so
completely was tranquillity restored by Brewster's lengthened illness.

The showers of April had passed, and on the
banks and hedge-rows primroses yet flou-
rished, and the scent of the violet told from
beneath its green retreat where its blossoms
were to be found. The birds sang merrily, as
they hopped from tree to tree, the streams ran
sparkling in the sun-beams, or darkly beneath
the over-hanging trees, and the sky, spread
above all, was as bright and serene as Mabel's
eyes. Her footstep was elastic as ever when she
walked along the meadows, and her heart was
glad. Jenkins loved her, and she well knew
how much she loved him. There was nothing
to oppose their love, and they yielded fully to
ts influences; every hour that Jenkins could
spare from his professional engagements he
spent with Mabel, losing as little time on the

road as possible. At first he never went without his lively friend Sawyer; after a few visits he ventured alone, and at length he purposely rode over when his rattle-brain associate was out of the way.

He had never spoken of love to Mabel, ever respecting the dark garments she wore, but both thoroughly understood each other's feelings and thoughts; no explanation was needed till the fitting time should arrive.

Mabel, though she often thought of her late husband with sadness and regret, had never been more happy in her life than she was now; Jenkins was, in truth, her first love. He was handsome, tender, joyous and merry, yet without frivolity, open, generous and unaffected. That he adored her without telling her so, was evidenced by his seeking every opportunity of pleasing her. What more could she need? She was her own mistress, and there was none to say "Nay, you shall not have him."

As for Jenkins he was the happiest of the happy. He laughed and joked with Willie Sawyer to Willie's heart's content. There were no more fits of abstraction, no more clouds of doubt, no more anger, no more vacant looks and long drawn sighs, no more dejection and hanging of head, no more pacings up and down the room, like a tiger pacing his den. Peter had none but happy thoughts to rest upon. He arose with glee, he went through his professional duties actively, gaily and cheerfully, he retired to rest, and slept like a light hearted man, free from worldly cares.

Brewster in the meanwhile was gradually recovering his strength, inhaling the sweet spring air, and regaining his usual sallow tinge in lieu of the livid white, which had been triumphing in his cheeks. All around, him wore the aspect of serenity and innocence. The lovely green meadows stretching beneath the bright sunshine; the cornfields with the young blades peeping forth; the quiet woods, the flocks and herds, the songs of birds, the labourers whistling and working, the angler proving his patience by the river side till he hooked his fish, the little rosy cheeked, curly-pated children, playing and shrieking out their mirth, and the whole catalogue of quiet country life; in none of these was there aught but innocence to be found.

Brewster walked along the meadows, or sauntered in the woods, the only guilty thing in that quiet spot. His mind was in contrast with all about him. He felt neither the beauties of the country, nor the balmy air, nor the placidity and calm of all around him. He had no thankfulness in his heart for his recovery from a sickness which had well nigh sent him from the world with all his sins upon him. He felt no repentance for his past life, nor did he make any resolutions for leading a better. He had but one thought—that was the fulfilment of his wishes regarding Mabel, and a resolve to take better care of himself for the future and avoid all causes of sickness.

He only awaited the perfect re-establishment of his health ere he re-commenced his designs upon the widow Silverton. He lay for hours on his back, on some warm sunny bank, his hat perched on his face to prevent the sun's rays shining upon it; and in those hours he meditated on his undying love and future plans, for fulfilling his desire. He was miserable as man could well be, languid and nervous, his mind wandering but not sufficiently so as to make him a confirmed maniac. At mid-day even he would see the spectre that haunted him; from behind the sturdy trunks of the trees he would see the old hag peep out and laugh, and chatter and grin at him, and feel her twitch his clothes as he passed. In the still warm air, when all was hushed at noon, save the distant tinkling of a sheep's bell, or the cuckoo's note, he heard a cold whisper close to his ear which said :—

" Renounce her ! "

Wherever Brewster looked, the cadaverous pallid face of Silverton was before him, shadowy and indistinct like a vapour, but still it was there, the glazed eyes fixed steadily upon him. He could not escape ; opiates and strong drinks were his resource, but they only aggravated his illusions. Jenkins watched him and delayed his return to town as much and as long as he possibly could. Brewster never spoke to him of Mabel, and when Jenkins named her he pretended not to hear, and commenced upon other topics. He looked upon Peter with the evil eye of jealousy and envy, and yet he clung to him. His nervous fears about his life, making him regard him as his only refuge and defence against death.

Mabel's peaceful life was drawing to a close. Her dreaded lover found himself sufficiently recovered to persecute her again. Without saying a word to Jenkins, one fine morning he transported himself to his delectable town residence, and, without a moment's delay, prepared to seek Mabel. His progress was arrested, however, by the person calling herself his cook and maid of all work.

" Your honour,"she said, " Thomas went off the day after you left, and I am not answerable for his evil deeds."

" How ? " asked Brewster.

" Your honor's great silver mugs be gone."

" Damnation ! " cried the Doctor in no gentletone, and running to his room he discovered that all the locks had been picked, and his money and plate all stolen.

Brewster had made a collection of most

precious unset diamonds which formed a con-
centrated species of property. The value of
these diamonds was great; large, polished,
sparkling stones, deposited in a small inner
casket, which in its turn was placed in a
secret drawer in his bureau. The drawer was
gaping open as if in astonishment at the
departure of its precious charge. Brewster
shook his clenched fist and stamped his foot.
How could Thomas have dreamed of the existence of that precious mine? Brewster had
revealed it in his delirium. He proceeded to
open a sliding side of the bureau concealing a
drawer which opened by a spring. In this
receptacle was coin to the amount of a thousand pounds, and that to his joy was safe;
but several other sums of money and precious
stones were gone, as well as silver tankards,
salt-cellars, and other articles of plate which
had from time to time been presented to him
by his patients.

In one of the drawers he found a letter ill-
folded and exceedingly dirty, addressed to
himself and sealed with wax, bearing the
impression of a thumb in the place of a seal.
The enraged Doctor seized and broke it open,
and owing to the bad writing and worse
spelling, to say nothing of innumerable blots
of ink, he read slowly the following choice
morceau.

" Master,

"I have taking all I could lay my
'ands on. What a fool you must be to get
yourself into a fever, and blab all your secrets.
Me and Doctor Jenkins noes all your secrets.
I thanks you for telling me ware to find your
treasures. I have took all I wants, and you
had better make yourself easy about I—and
not try to ketch me, for, if you do, by the
Lord Harry I will tell all I know and bring
you to the gallus, ware you daserve to
swing. If you lets me alone, I will let you

alone and your secrets ull be safe. So mind.

"I wish you luck with the pretty wider. Doctor Jenkins loves hur quite as much as you does, and I can tell you, he's ever so much andsomer a man than you be, and will win hur. Farewell, old crazy master. You had better give up courting the wider, and spending good time for nothing, but set to work again in arnest, and make up what I have eased you of.

"Your very umble servant,

"Thomas Huggins."

Rage was dominant in Brewster's breast. He commenced drumming with his knuckles on the table, and then threw himself into his chair, and re-perused the precious document. He however found nothing in it that could any way comfort him, for his hoarded wealth had disappeared, and what was worse, Thomas knew his great secret, and he felt that he was completely in his power. Jenkins too, knew of his hidden deeds, and his hatred took a tenfold violence against him. "That fellow marry Mabel! Curse him, never!" cried Brewster, and closing the bureau with extreme violence, and tearing the letter into hundreds of pieces, he rushed out of the room.

"Please Doctor what would you like to have got ready for your dinner?" asked the cook, who met him in the passage.

"The devil and all his imps!" shouted Brewster rushing past her into the street. On he went, taking no heed of those whom he met. His wild look created a smile with some, pity with others; some looked grave, whilst others laughed; many censured him; but he neither saw the people nor heard their comments. He ran at his utmost speed till he at length, out of breath, reached Mrs. Silverton's town house. He gave a thundering knock at the door, and as soon as the servant opened it, rushed past him, mounted the stairs two at a time, and without knock-ing or waiting, rushed into Mabel's usual sitting-room, where he found the amiable step-daughter sitting in a gloomy reverie. This sudden entrance of the doctor caused her to shriek and·run the needle into her finger instead of the work she held.

"Where is Mabel?" he cried, in a hoarse voice : all his former caution forgotten, in his terrible rage and unsound state of mind.

"Oh! Doctor Brewster, you have alarmed me so dreadfully that—"

"Where is Mabel?" he repeated, gazing upon her, literally foaming at the mouth, his eyes almost starting from their sockets.

The maiden pushed back her chair, which unfortunately caught the leg of a horrible little cur for which she had great affection. The animal yelled loudly.

"Where is Mabel?" again shouted Brewster at the top of his voice.

"In the country," cried the lady taking up her pet and running from the room.

Brewster made no attempt at detaining her. He stood a minute or two apparently lost in thought, but suddenly, as if some fresh idea had taken possession of his mind, he hurried from the house into the street, and without looking either to the right or to the left regained his house, put on a pair of rusty spurs, saddled the swiftest horse he possessed, and having put the bit into its mouth, after some indignant tossings of its head, mounted the awkward brute, and once in the highway, he dashed his spurs into the animal's sides, and away flew horse and rider to the great danger of the latter.

The enraged Doctor arrived at Mrs. Silverton's country house, and hastily dismounting asked for the mistress.

"She went out for a walk some time since," the servant respectfully answered.

"Alone?"

"Yes, sir."

"Which way?"

"I think she took the road across the meadow to the right."

"Let my horse be put into the stable, and a feed of corn given to him."

"Yes, sir."

"Across the meadow to the right, I believe you said."

"Yes sir, towards the wood."

The wood was some half mile or more from the house, a very pleasant walk on a hot, sunny day, a walk which the former possessor of the estate was very fond of taking. At the end of the wood ran a clear, sparkling stream, with overhanging branches, forming a sort of canopy on which the birds sang merrily. A rustic chair had been placed on the bank, and there Mr. and Mrs. Silverton used frequently to spend their time in reading and listening to the rippling water and the sweet songs of the birds.

To this spot Mabel had taken her book, and sat sheltered from the scorching sun. The book was one Jenkins had lent to her, and on its margin several pencilled remarks had been made by him. She kept her eyes steadily on the volume, but her thoughts at times wandered to its handsome and agreeable owner, whom she expected to see in the evening. Pleasing remembrances of past visits, words and tender looks, all bearing love's impress, and the joyous anticipation of their speedy repetition rendered Mabel's face the reflex of her glad heart; her smile was bright as the sun, and her whole soul was in unison with the scene around her.

In this transport of love and happiness, Brewster beheld her, whilst, hidden from her sight. The soft turf had prevented his footsteps being heard. Mabel, as she sat, little thought how near her tormentor was standing with his arms folded over his chest, his eyes glaring at her, and his thin lips wreathed into a sardonic smile.

Brewster neither spoke nor moved—he looked up, and the shadowy face of Silverton was there, as ever before him. The old hag too, put out her shrivelled arm and pointed with her long bony finger to Mabel.

"I defy you both," he mentally exclaimed, at the same time shaking his clenched hand, and in the next instant he was seated beside Mabel, and seizing her hand pressed it passionately to his lips.

Mabel lost all power of speech ; she endeavoured to rise, but Brewster with a firm grasp detained her.

"My dear Mabel," he said in his softest

voice and trying to look most tenderly. " You must not leave me.   Have you not heard that I have been nearly at death's door?"

" I am truly sorry to hear it," she said in trembling accents ; and she again attempted to get away from him.

"Oh Mabel! but for the thought of you, my malady would have killed me.   Day and night your sweet face was my constant companion—my only consoler.   Dearest Mabel, do you love me?   Why do you tremble—why do you try to get away from me.   I will not let you quit me.   There is no need of trembling, I love you beyond all on earth or in heaven.   Do you love me in return?"

" I regard you as one of my true friends," replied Mabel, making an effort to master her fears, but she dared not trust her eyes to look upon her companion.

" Is that all, sweet love" he said, again pressing her hand.   " It is not so that I would have you love me. You must love me as your lover and ere long become my wife. Will you not answer me."

The last words were uttered sharply, and with much asperity, and Mabel felt him pull her arm somewhat roughly. She could not answer; and Brewster again put the question in a somewhat fierce tone and very impatiently.

"Doctor Brewster," she at length said scarcely above a whisper, "You know I cannot."

" Why not ?" he asked; and without waiting for her reply he went on. "I can tell you why you cannot. You have listened to the false speeches of Peter Jenkins and placed your affections upon him."

Mabel blushed crimson, and a moment after turned ashy pale. Brewster looked scornfully, laughed demoniacally and then again spoke.

"Listen to me, Mabel. I do not care for your love. I only ask you to become my

wife. Love will assuredly follow. Will you
wed me?"

"Never!"

"Then take the consequences, thou silly
fool," cried Brewster with the voice and look
of a demon. "I swear by heaven and hell, if
you persevere in your love for Jenkins, I will
slay him. Refuse to become my wife at your
peril. I will torment and persecute you till
you yield. So you had better give me your
promise at once. Will you be my wife?"

"I cannot," she replied, her heart beating
violently and her kness trembling beneath her
so that she could scarcely move.

"You cannot!—You can if you will and
what's more you shall!"

So saying, with his right hand he seized her
throat and held the back of her head tightly
with the other.

"If you scream or attempt to stir, I will
strangle you," he said in a suppressed voice,

whilst the birds were singing above and the water gurgling below as if no persecuting tyrant were there.

"Promise to be my wife!" he went on "and beware that you say not a word of what has passed to Jenkins, if you do I vow solemnly I will murder both. Once more, I ask, will you be mine?"

Mabel felt the hand tighten on her soft white throat. She uttered a faint cry.

"Silence!" he roared, looking like a wild beast at the trembling woman in his grasp.

"Have mercy on me," she said, "dear Dr. Brewster, do not harm me, I entreat you to release me."

"Tell me that you will be mine," and he gave her throat another gripe.

"I defy you both!" he continued, laughing in a most extraordinary manner, and looking defiantly at his phantom visions.

Mabel felt that her strength was fast failing.

Her head was becoming dizzy, and her eyes were almost closed. Suddenly a joyous bark was heard, and the crackling of dry branches. In another instant her faithful dog bounded through the underwood and stood beside his mistress, for whom he had been searching.

The presence of her dog gave her fresh courage, for she felt now if she had a noble protector.

"Seize him, good dog," she cried, as loudly as she could, "seize him!"

With a growl and then a bark the dog darted at Brewster, and held him fast.

It was now his turn to pray, but there was nobody to pray to. Mabel had darted off at her utmost speed, whilst the dog as if divining his mistress's thoughts, held the enraged and terrified doctor until she was out of danger; and then looking fiercely at him, let go his hold and ran off at full speed after his kind mistress.

CHAPTER IX.

In the evening when Jenkins paid his promised visit he found Mabel pale, greatly agitated and absent. With his experienced eye, although she received him with her usual fondness of both look and smile, he at once detected that her thoughts were wandering upon something else beside himself. He was at a loss to guess the meaning of all this. He was not aware that Brewster had returned to town from the country. Never for a moment dreaming that he had only a short time before

left the farm, and had ridden like a madman
along the same road he had taken. Jenkins
had missed him, having found out a short cut
by means of which, and by leaping a hedge
and a couple of ditches, he arrived nearly
half-an-hour earlier.

It was about two hours after Mabel's rencontre with Brewster, when Jenkins appeared,
and her agitation and terror had but little
abated.

When Jenkins took her hand, however, she
felt a degree of safety, and she would instantly
have told him all the insults she had undergone at the hands of Brewster, had she not
recollected the dreadful vengeance he had so
solemnly sworn. It might be only a vague
threat, yet she thought, in his madness,
he was capable of killing his rival. Jenkins'
visit, therefore, did not afford all the pleasure it
should have done. Unfortunately he was
obliged to return to town much earlier than

he otherwise would have done to attend a patient
who was very seriously ill, besides which
they neither of them seemed quite at ease.
Mabel endeavouring to behave as usual, and by
her efforts to do so giving an embarrassment
to her manner, which Jenkins perceived ; she
at the same time feeling certain that he
remarked it, and longed to know the cause of
her embarrassment, yet not venturing to
ask her. They parted tenderly, and Jenkins
rode off pondering on what had occurred,
leaving Mabel full of fears, and turning over
in her mind whether it would be better to tell
him all that occurred during the late rencontre
with Brewster, or to maintain a strict silence.

Mabel was bewildered, and knew not what
course to pursue. Once she thought of
calling to her aid her cousin, Willie Sawyer,
but she almost instantly rejected the suggestion fearing he would use some rash

violence, which would involve them all in trouble.

As the twilight came on, her fears redoubled, and she felt exceeding loneliness in the large old house. She sat at her window watching the flitting bats, and looking towards the meadows; she thought she saw the figure of Brewster peering through the bushes, and as the light wind rustled the leaves, she fancied she heard him stealthily creeping towards the house. At length she rang for lights, as the only remedy for her nervous fears, and before going to the upper part of the house, to her bed-room, she ordered that all the doors might at once be locked and barred; she searched her room, looking into every closet, and under the bed, so fearful was she that Brewster might have returned and, unperceived, entered the house and hidden himself there.

Mabel was not disposed to sleep, and long

sat reading. She had no friend near her, none but servants, and it was quite out of the question to call her old valet to bear her company. The consequence was she remained and listening till she was afraid almost to speak or stir : the silence only now and then being interrupted by the rats running up the walls, which set her heart beating as quickly as if Brewster himself had tumbled into the room. The upshot of all this was, that she undressed as speedily as possible, threw herself into bed, and like a frightened child pulled the clothes over her head and went to sleep to the loud beating of her heart, and forgot both Jenkins and Brewster till the morning.

Then the remembrance of the rencontre of the previous day returned with fresh fears. She expected the arrival of Brewster every minute; her pleasant walks through the meadows were at an end, she so dreaded the idea of meet-

ing him when at any distance from home. She
wandered about her garden, read, worked and
tried to forget him: but his sardonic look
and horrid threats, were not to be driven from
her mind by any effort, and consequently
every hour she found herself getting more
frightened and more nervous. She never for
a moment allowed her faithful dog to leave
her side; feeling great faith in his strong
frame, huge paws, large teeth and shaggy
coat, not to mention the tender upturning of
his patient eyes, when she patted his head and
talked to him; then and then only did she feel
the sensation of perfect security.

The dog at those moments was everything
to his mistress, and the animal seeming
to be perfectly conscious that his services were
required, patiently gave up his accustomed long rambles about the neighbouring
fields and meadows, to lie down quietly by
her side, striking the floor every now and then

with his feathery tail whenever he saw her soft eyes cast upon him.

Brewster, as may readily be imagined, was meditating another attack. At times, when his mind was free from its hallucinations, he looked upon the past and could but be aware of the miserable position in which his bad passions had placed him. He was regarded by the public as a madman, and he consequently was without a single patient. His property had been carried off by his dishonest servant ; Mabel he was convinced loved Jenkins : and he was most miserable. His mind, too, was enfeebled, he was haunted by fearful visions, especially when the darkness of night began ; he was just capable of perceiving that there was a precipice before him down which he did not dare to look.

Still, in his madness, Brewster loved Mabel, and despite all the evils that passion brought him, and all that he had suffered, and was still suffering, he felt a something, which he could not define, urging him forward to win her. His nights were passed in the most painful terror, sleep for hours was unknown to him, and only when nature became exhausted did he fall into a troubled slumber. He tried opiates, but they had lost their effect. Instead of sleep they only produced an amount of excitement terrible to contemplate, multiplied his visions and made his madness triumphant. The poor old woman who acted as cook, housemaid and maid of all work, at first was horrified at his wild ravings, but after a time she got accustomed to them, and, as soon as she knew he had retired to bed, she locked him in his room till morning.

Some days had elapsed since Brewster had made his appearance at Mrs. Silverton's country house; the fear of her dog's sharp teeth, flashing eyes, and powerful frame had subsided, and he again set forth to pour

out his love to the widow. She was walking
in her garden and had just taken courage to
reward her dog's faithfulness and enduring
patience by sending him for a ramble by
himself. No sooner was the word given than
off he bounded, barking and wagging his tail,
whilst his mistress gazed fondly after him.

Jenkins had not failed in his daily visits,
and each day had found her sad, absent,
and constrained. That very morning he had
parted from her wondering what could possibly have caused the sadness and absence
of mind which possessed her. He was a clear-
sighted man, and could generally set things
down to their causes, but on this occasion his
mind became warped by passion, and when
that is the case, poor human creatures have
but little chance.

Passion took possession of him, and he made
up his mind that Mabel had never truly loved
him, or if she had, had become tired of him,

or that in some way or other he had offended
her. Hereupon he unwisely took passion into
his counsels, and first grew sad, then enraged,
then both; first he allowed his horse to go at
snail's pace, then to gallop off furiously; first
he swore that he did not care a pinch of snuff
for her, then that he adored her; he said
to himself there were plenty of other women
in the world besides her, and then that she was
the only one he had or ever could love. He
was growing from bad to worse, from a rational
lover to a silly madman, when reason once
more asserted her right, his horse was pulled
up and made to canter gently, he smoothed
his brow, and putting his fingers through his
hair, began to reflect that Mabel might have
many causes for sorrow, absence and constraint.
He began to argue rationally with himself and
discovered he had suffered passion to make
a puppet of him. He called himself an idiot
—a fool, and unjust to the lady of his love,

and by the time he reached home he was quiet
and composed, and with the conviction on his
mind that he might have done quite as well
or better without going through such a hurly-
burly.

Lovers, take advice from Jenkins, and do
not let passion get the better of your judgment, and run through your breasts like a
mad-dog, making you rabid—blind and per-
verse.

Mabel as we said was walking in her garden ;
stopping now and then to admire some fresh
blooming flower, and after awhile she gained
the terrace from which she could survey
the whole face of the country. The sky was
partially obscured and heavy-looking clouds
were driving towards her, but other and lighter
and brighter clouds gave relief to the darker.
The evening sun shone upon the spot where
she stood, but the country was in gloom
beneath the rolling clouds. The air was warm

and close, and everything denoted a coming storm. The birds had given over their singing and were hopping about and settling themselves for the night among the thick bushes and branches, and the peacocks spread out their tails, as they stood on the wall of the terrace, shining in the crimson sunbeams like gold. The lowing of the cattle in the distant meadows was pleasantly heard through the still air, whilst the dark clouds came steadily rolling up as if in battle array to send forth their thunder and lightning. Mabel left the terrace, walked quickly towards to the house, and went to her solitary room where the last rays of the setting sun shone on the wall, making the rest look more dark and dismal. Mabel, as was her wont, sat down opposite the portrait of her husband, on which she fixed her eyes. His seemed to meet hers tenderly and lovingly as ever. She smiled on the portrait, but the smile gave way to a faint cry as a hand was placed on her shoulder. She turned round and at the back of her chair, to her horror and dismay, Brewster stood looking, or rather attempting to look lovingly at her.

"Why did you scream, my dear Mabel?" he said, holding out his hand, "I have been waiting patiently for you some time."

This was true, he had been in the parlour for a considerable time, but Mabel when she entered did not see him, her eyes having been somewhat dazzled by the setting sun. Poor Mabel's heart beat violently and she trembled from head to foot, such effect had the presence of Brewster upon her. She was unable to utter a word.

"Your lover will not come to visit you to-night," said Brewster, taking her unresisting hand, "and as there is a storm coming on, I will bear you company and talk to you of my devoted love till it be past."

He took a chair beside her, and tightly

grasping her hand gazed at her as if he would read her every thought, noting the terror and aversion that seemed to paralyse his victim.

" Have you reflected on my words since we parted ? " he asked, bending towards her.

" Yes," she said, in a faint voice, not daring to look at him.

" That's right ; and you have determined to be my wife—and to think no more of that dissolute spendthrift Jenkins, who only seeks your money."

A flash of lightning darted through the room. Brewster started and Mabel ran towards the door. He followed, and putting his arms round her waist held her fast.

"No, no, my sweet love, I cannot let you go. I love you too well for that," and he pressed his lips upon her forehead, whilst she felt utterly powerless in his grasp.

"Go on and prosper," sounded in his ears,

and Brewster's eyes flashed and his grasp became tighter round Mabel's waist. He saw
the old hag who was nodding and smiling at
him, whilst she extended her shrivelled arm
and pointed with her long bony fingers. "Go
on, go on, your time is short, the Devil will
have you shortly. Go on, and prosper! ha!
ha! ha!"

She began to sing in her cracked voice and
the approaching thunder pealed out an accom-
paniment. Mabel looked at her tyrant's
glaring eyes, as he still held her in his iron
grasp.

"The devil and all his imps take you! I
defy you all! She shall be mine!" and he
stamped angrily with his foot. "Yes, yes,
laugh on, you wretched, withered old hag.
She shall be my wife!"

"We shall soon be in the infernal regions,"
she cried, "too good a place for a murderer,
your hours are numbered: make haste Doctor

—make haste, your time for making love is short—take your kisses whilst you can, ha! ha! ha!"

"Get out of my sight, you fury!" he exclaimed passionately.

Mabel's consciousness did not leave her, Brewster's firm hold round her waist kept her from falling; she saw his wild, wandering eyes and heard his strange words, and felt that she was in the power of a madman.

After a moment's delay he let go her waist and took both her hands in his, saying, "My beloved Mabel—my lovely Mabel. Speak once for all. Tell me, will you be my wife? —will you be only mine?"

"Never."

"Never! that's a long while, darling," he said again kissing her; and then with the look of a demon he continued: "Say that you will give up Jenkins and marry me. If you will not promise this, I swear by the lightning and the thunder he shall be a dead man in less than twenty-four hours. May the lightning strike me dead if he be not ! "

At the instant a most vivid flash of lightning and a loud peal of thunder startled both the tyrant and his victim.

A violent fit of tears came to Mabel's relief, and she said :

'Doctor Brewster, I beseech you to have mercy on me. I cannot love you as you would wish, and without love I never could be yours."

"Fool ! idiot ! what's the use of tears unless they be shed to water Jenkins' grave. Die he shall. I solemnly swear it ! Say but the words 'I love you ' and he shall live ! "

" Never ! "

" Never ! " he echoed.

" Leave me," she cried. " Let me beg of you to leave me."

" Never ! "

VOL. II.   K

Brewster seized her throat as he had done once before.

"Will you be my wife? ha! ha! ha!— will you be mine?" and he pressed his fingers tighter.

"Yes! in a twinkling" said a merry voice outside the window. It was Willie Sawyer who spoke; he had been watching the love-making at the window, through which he had intended entering to frighten his cousin, and had thus witnessed the whole of Brewster's method of courting.

The words were no sooner uttered, than Willie squeezed his fat person through the window, and in an instant the mad Doctor was in his grip.

"You miserable wretch! You cowardly hound!" he cried.

Brewster let go his hold of Mabel, and she sank almost fainting into a chair, watching anxiously the proceedings of her cousin and her persecutor.

" I overheard the whole of your vile threats, you cowardly wretch," cried Willie shaking the trembling Brewster violently, " and I will make you beg pardon.—Down on your knees you cur." ·

And instantly the Doctor was forced on his knees.

The wretched man made no attempt at resistance, neither did he speak.

Sawyer held his heavy whip above Brewster's head, and without another word gave him five or six cuts as hard as he could strike, Brewster screaming at each blow; and after a severe blow on the miserable man's face, he gave him a violent kick which prostrated him on his face at the other side of the room.

Mabel had used her gentle persuasion that

her cousin should spare her persecutor but in vain.

" Spare the vermin ! you silly little goose " cried Sawyer. " I'll teach the hound better manners. Get up, you vile scamp ! "

Brewster obeyed, and Sawyer with another lash of the whip seized him by one of his ears, led him, or rather dragged him to the door—opening which, he let go his ear, and taking him by the back of his neck forced him towards the stables, where he found his horse ready saddled and bridled.

" Up you vile lump of deformity ! " he cried. " Mount and ride to the devil ! "

Brewster tremblingly obeyed, as far as mounting was concerned.

Sawyer still held the bridle, as he said :—

" Let this be a warning to you. If you ever utter another word of what you call love to my cousin, or write a single line to her, I will repeat this dose, (you see I speak professionally,) with tenfold strength—so now be off, and may the devil hunt you through the storm. Farewell you love-making beauty, go home and hug your tender shoulders to-night. Away!" and with another slash upon the wretched man's shoulders, and another upon his horse, he let go his hold of the bridle.

The horse reared and snorted under the heavy blow, and Brewster was scarcely able to keep his seat. Finding himself at liberty, he began cursing Sawyer with all the hard words he could find, and seizing a pistol, which he had placed in the holster of the saddle, he fired at Sawyer, and dashing spurs into his horse's sides rode off without turning his head to see what had been the result of his pistol-shot.

Fortunately the rearing of the horse had made Brewster's aim unsteady, and the bullet instead of entering Sawyer's head lodged in the stable door.

"Well meant," cried Willie, "but 'twas sad waste of powder and ball."

Away flew horse and rider.

"Wretch! where do you expect to roost after death! Poor Mabel!" continued Sawyer looking after horse and rider till they were out of sight.

He returned to the house where he found Mabel solacing herself as best she could by crying bitterly. She did not hear him enter the room, and was not aware of his presence till he took hold of one of her ears.

"Hallo!" he cried. "Don't shed any more tears. I have sent the brute off, and I'll be bound he'll not come back again in a hurry to make such loving speeches; ugh! the vermin!—I gave him such a slashing over his shoulders, as will last him for a week to come.

Besides I've spoilt his beauty with the blow on his face—the cowardly sneaking devil!"

"Oh, Willie, have you not been too harsh with him?"

"Harsh! he deserves a thousand-fold the punishment I inflicted. Why, the fiend fired his pistol at me, instead of defending himself like a man. Fortunately his horse reared and the ball went into the door instead of my head."

This brought all Mabel's fears back again. If he would fire at her cousin he would not hesitate to murder Doctor Jenkins, as he had more than once threatened he would. She almost fainted at the thought, and turned pale as death.

Sawyer perceived the change that came over her face.

"What is it, Mabel?"

Forgetting everything but the dreadful idea of Jenkins being murdered by Brewster, she told her cousin all that had happened. She gave him a full account of Brewster's persecution and threats, and the misery she had of late endured, when Jenkins visited her, and her dread at parting from him.

"Oh! Willie, will you help me?" she said in a piteous tone.

"You seem to take great interest in Peter Jenkins. I've long suspected there was something stronger than friendship going on. Come, you silly, frightened dove! Be candid with me. Do you love him?"

Mabel cast her eyes upon the floor, and scarcely knew how to answer. She felt that, in her anxiety, she had betrayed herself.

"Come, Mabel, out with it. Do you love Peter, or do you not!"

"No!" said Mabel faintly.

"No's a lie, you little deceiver—you can't deceive me, with your faintly uttered 'No' which I am certain means 'yes.' Come, coz.

try again. Do you love Peter—yes or no!"

"Well then, Willie dear, yes!"

"Hurra!—hurra!" cried Willie catching her in his arms and giving her a kiss. "That's right, my darling, fair and above board. Spoken like a true woman! The moment the rain ceases and the storm has past, I'll be off to Peter and put him on his guard, before that black devil can either poison or put his dissecting knife between his ribs."

It was not long ere the storm and the rain ceased, and Sawyer gave his cousin another kiss, and was on his horse scampering back to town. His delight knew no bounds; he whistled, he sang snatches of all his best and most humorous songs—he talked to his horse in the most loving terms, at the same time belabouring him with a lash of his whip. As he thus rode through the various villages and hamlets on the road, he roused the sleepers

from their beds to see what could be the matter, and to ascertain who was the songster at
such a time of night. Willie, however, heeded
them not, his only thought was the pleasure
he was about to impart to his long tried friend
Jenkins.

On his arrival at Jenkins' house, all the
household had retired to rest, and he began
thundering away at the door with the handle
of his whip. In a minute or two a window
was thrown up, and Peter called out " who's
there."

" Who's there !" echoed Sawyer, " who
should be here, but myself."

" Sawyer ! "

" Yes—be quick man and let me in. I
come upon a matter of life and death ! "

Jenkins closed his window, and, speedily as
he could, dressed himself, Sawyer the while
singing out some appropriate love song.

In an incredible short time, Jenkins opened the door, and Billy having heard Sawyer's voice, brought a lanten and went with Sawyer to the stable.

When Willie returned to the house, he found his master and Sawyer laughing, and in high spirits—and was told to put out supper, and to get wine and grog out.

Sawyer in the interim had related to his friend Peter, all that had happened at Mabel's country house, winding up the narrative with Mabel's "yes."

"Nonsense, Willie!"

"By Jove! nonsense enough for such a pretty dear to fall in love with such an ugly owl as you—but it's true for all that."

Jenkins was in the seventh heaven, and urged his friend to eat, drink, and be merry; and truly enough Willie played his part to perfection; he ate enough, he drank enough,

he talked enough and he sang enough—and
in his exhilaration set fire to Billy's hair,
and by way of making amends gave him some
gold coins.   In this manner the night was
ended.

CHAPTER X.

Let us follow Brewster for awhile. His rage knew no bounds: he gallopped off as hard as his high-boned horse could carry him, hoping he had either killed or wounded Sawyer. In his present state of mind he cared not which.

The black clouds were above him casting a dark shadow upon the earth. The sun had set and the twilight had passed into night: the lightning flashed more frequently, and the thunder claps grew louder and louder whilst the rain began to fall heavily.

The horse went at full speed but its master's

mind went more rapidly still. The visions of his victim's ashy rigid face met him wherever he turned his eyes—and he cursed, and once or twice struck at the fancied phantom. Still the face was there, white and ghastly pale.

" Curse you ! stare away ! " Brewster cried " I am not afraid of you—I defy you, so stare away as much as you like. Ha ! ha ! ha ! your wife shall soon be my wife ! ha ! ha ! "

On he rode heeding not the vivid flashes of the lightning nor the long loud rolling of the thunder. Furiously dashed along the road both horse and rider, neither apparently heeding the storm.

It was not very long, however, ere the horse slackened its pace. Brewster's rage had become calmer, his heart began to fail him, and, in the place of rage, fear and trembling took possession of him.

Every flash of lightning seemed to bring before his eyes that stern pale face, and in the

darkness that followed each flash, the rever-
berating thunder brought to his ears the
groans and screams of the hag, singing above
the crash of the elements in her screeching
voice

"Come along! come along!"

After one terrific clap of thunder, the horse
snorted, reared, plunged, and at length went
off at its utmost speed. Brewster tried to
restrain the animal, but the more he tugged
at the bridle the faster became its flight. He
felt a hand seize his stirrup, and the next flash
of lightning showed him the old hag, holding
on by it and running by his side—her white
hair flying about her head and breast, and her
eyes glaring up at him fearfully.

"Spur away! faster and faster! The devil
and all his imps are abroad, this beautiful
night. So you won't marry the lovely Mabel,
you won't kiss the timid woman. You
thought she'd love you, and wed you!

you killed her old husband and fitted yourself for the devil! and he'll have you. There's no escape! Whip and spur, the faster the better!"

Brewster uttered shriek after shriek, but his voice was drowned in the storm raging above. "Mercy! mercy!—Do but let me live. I will atone for all my evil deeds— mercy! mercy!"

"Spur on and hold your peace," cried the hag, "it's too late—it's too late! Why did you murder the poor old man?—It's too late! Spur on, spur on."

Brewster could see by the flashes of light- ning that his horse was carrying him across the open country over a large heath. Was he to die there? His soul sickened more and more at every flash of the electric fluid. He tried to shut out the whole scene by closing his eyes, but a fresh flash made him open them again; the air appeared filled with spectres piled one above the other; look which way he would he was hemmed in by a dense troop of demons.

Was his life coming to a close? Were his evil deeds going to meet their punishment? From his youth upwards the sins he had committed rose before him, clearly and distinctly, as though each had been only just achieved, and each gave a severe stab to his conscience. What was Mabel to him then? Could she save him! He tried to throw himself from his horse but the hag held him on with supernatural strength.

"Patience! patience! You will soon be there. Do you see yon tall oak? Make for that—We shall meet again, good night and a merry journey."

She vanished. The spectres too had all disappeared, even the face of the dead was no longer seen.

"My mind has been wandering" he said, "and I have lost my road."

He tried to turn his horse, but it went full gallop towards the gigantic oak which stood in solitary grandeur in the middle of the heath.

Brewster was silent, but the storm raging in his soul surpassed that of the heavens. His conscience thundered in his breast, and remorse like lightning scorched his heart. He was alone. If he was to die, there was none to help him. Had there been thousands, could they have saved him? He felt as though the hand of death was upon him, and as the lightning flashed it revealed a countenance, a guilty coward countenance too horrible for man to have looked upon, a countenance full of despair, of fear, of agony, a face so sharp, so rigid, more like that of a spectre than of a man.

The horse bore Brewster to the oak. He

tried in vain to turn him from it. He reached it, and stood snorting and pawing the earth beneath its wide spread branches. The rider sat as rigid as a statue.

"I am dying," passed in a whisper between his burning lips. He continued to repeat the words, but he scarcely believed them. He felt as if he were in a trance. He looked steadily on the flashes of lightning; he listened calmly to the pealing of the thunder, and to the pelting hail, but seemed not to feel its cutting stones.

"I am dying," he continued, "I am dying —I am dying!"

Despair took possession of him, he yelled: he tore his hair: put spurs to his horse and strove to fly. The horse reared and pawed the wet earth, but refused to move.

"Save me—save me!" shouted Brewster. His voice seemed unearthly as it rang over the heath. No ear heard his cry: he was alone with his guilt.

Suddenly the rain and hail ceased. Brewster's heart beat almost to bursting, it's work was nearly over. A cold shiver ran through his veins. He let go the reins, and hid his face in his hands. Scalding tears were in his eyes—and thought was suspended.

Anon the dense mass of clouds opened, and the flaring bolt fell, striking the top of the majestic oak, which came to the earth with a fearful crash, crushing the wretched man and his horse beneath its blackened branches,— but neither horse nor rider were sensible of the loud, deafening thunder that instantaneously followed the bolt; neither of them heard it bound, and roll, and break from cloud to cloud, they did not hear the mighty rush of wind, nor the pelting hail, though it bounded and danced upon them. Both were lying scorched and blackened—dead, at the foot of the shattered oak.

It was not long ere the storm ceased, and the thunder alone could be heard in the distance, and the sky was studded with stars, and the moon broke forth, shining on the bodies of the horse and his rider. The rain drops from the remaining branches of the oak pattered upon them. The morning sun rose resplendently, the birds sang merrily above them, and the carrion crows pounced down and fed upon them. Brewster felt them not. Where was his soul?

The storm of the night had cleared the atmosphere, which all the previous day had been hot and sultry. Now all was clear and bright. In truth it was a lovely morning, and beneath the high calm sky, and the hot sun lay all that remained of Brewster, unheeded and alone.

Beneath that same sky, and blazing sun

Peter Jenkins and Willie Sawyer were trotting their horses towards the country residence of Mrs. Silverton. The former having determined to urge Mabel to become, without further delay, his wife. Sawyer told his friend Peter that he had made up his mind not to 'spoil sport,' but that while he was angling for a wife, he would go fishing for pike, as his fishing tackle was all ready for him at his cousin's.

"Well, Peter, my lad, I wish you good luck," he said as they neared the house, " but I fear the demure little dissenter, will not consent to ' take you for better or for worse,' till the poor old husband has been underground a year and a day. However, you have a winning tongue, and a tolerably good looking figure—and upon my life, now I look at you, you have set yourself off to the best advantage,—go in and win, old fellow." ·

"I will do my best depend on it," replied

Jenkins with a smile, "and at the end of the day, we shall see who has proved the best angler."

"So be it," observed Sawyer, "here we are. Hallo! hallo! hurrah!" he cried as they rode into the stable yard and dismounted. A groom came grinning at Sawyer's hallooing, and took their horses, and the two friends walked to the house.

Poor Jenkins was terribly disappointed, for Mabel, worn out with fatigue, fright, and anxiety, still slept, and after waiting a couple of hours she still slept, so he had no alternative but to return to town without seeing her, whilst Sawyer took his tackle, and proceeded to the river.

"I shall be home in good time this evening, Peter, and bring some fish for supper, so get up your appetite, and I will bring you good tidings of the drowsy dormouse."

Sawyer was as good as his word. He caught

some fine fish. He did not forget, in the
middle of the day, to recruit his inner man;
he sat under the shade of some trees by the
water's edge, and sang and ate, and was as
merry as a cricket, and towards the evening
put up his fishing tackle, and went back to
his cousin's house. He found that she was
still in bed. He left her a portion of the fish,
together with the following letter, and rode to
town.

"SLEEPING BEAUTY! "

" Two handsome fellows intend calling
upon you early to-morrow, one especially the
pink of perfection, so be up and stirring
early..

"I leave you some fish for your refreshment.
Don't bother your head about the mad wretch
I belaboured so charmingly yesterday. Dream,

either awake or asleep, or both, of another who will offer you his—

" Good bye, I am off,

" Your loving coz.,

" WILLIE SAWYER."

Singing and whistling Sawyer left the house, and mounted his horse; and in less than five minutes was on his way to town, as full of animal spirits as the basket slung to his back was full of fish. He began soliloquising as to what he should do when he got to Jenkins' house, devising sundry methods of tormenting his friend.

" By Jove ! " he said, " I will put on a long face, and tell him that his lady-love is sinking very fast." Quite professional that !

ha! ha! ha! This fearful calamity having been brought on by the loving grip of his mad rival! I'll urge him to start off to-night, as soon as the fish can possibly be cooked and eaten. Poor Peter! his appetite will be none of the best. He'll be for starting forthwith, but I will delay him, by some means; and when I find him up to concert pitch and the supper ready, I'll undeceive him, and we will make a jolly supper and plenty of grog."

He had ridden about four miles, when his soliloquy was brought to a close, by the narrow road he was traversing being blocked up by a waggon and horses, and some labouring men walking on either side of the waggon.

Hallo! my fine fellows," he cried, "what's in the wind eh?"

" Good evening, Sar!" said one.

" Servant, Sar!" said another.

The same salutation being spoken by the

rest, the man who had the waggon and horses in charge, stopped them and said :—

"As we were going to our work this morning, that is Bill Somers and I, we fell in with a man and horse, lying stark dead, under the big oak on the heath. There be no doubt whatsomever, that a thunder bolt had struck the top of the oak and shivered the branches, which fell and killed the man and horse, who to my way of thinking had got under the oak for shelter from the tempest. No sooner had Bill and I seen how things stood, than we fetched a waggon and horses, and with the help of some of the other men who come up, we got the body of the man into the waggon, and are taking him to farmer Stern's barn. The nag will be fetched presently."

"Do you know who the man is?" asked Sawyer.

"No: we don't none of us know him. He's

L 3

terribly blackened."

"Let me have a look at him. Perhaps I may know him," said Willie, the idea flashing across his mind that it might perhaps be the wretched Brewster.

The men uncovered the body.

Sawyer rode close up to the waggon, and as he looked on the blackened body, he exclaimed :—

"Good heaven!"

"Do you know him, Sar? We never saw him afore."

"Do I know him? to be sure I do. I parted from him last evening."

There was no mistaking the identity of the corpse, Sawyer looked upon Brewster, whose face was frightfully distorted and discoloured. The discolouration seemed to proceed from a blow, and Sawyer shuddered as he remembered the one he had given him. The clothes, and upper part of the body were black and scorched, but the lower part scarcely touched. Both his eyes were gone, evidently plucked out by the crows. His hands were tightly clasped.

Sawyer's spirits for once sank, and he looked sorrowfully upon the dead body of the man he had so often annoyed by his mad pranks. For some time, he was silent, and seemed to have lost the power of speech, the scene of the previous evening coming vividly across his mind.

" Heaven forgive me ! " he murmured. " I am sorry I lashed the poor wretch so severely though he richly deserved the chastisement. How fearful has been his end ! "

At length the man who had been spokesman before said :—

" Pray, Sar, who may he be ? I hope he baint any of your relations, Sar. You seem so mighty taken aback."

" No, no, my good fellow, he is no relation of

mine, but I was at school with him, and have known him pretty well all my life. It is the body of Doctor Brewster."

"Doctor Brewster!" was echoed by all the men in attendance.

"Yes, and I think the wisest thing that can be done, will be to take the body to his residence in London."

This proposition met with the entire concurrence of the whole party, and the waggon moved on, Sawyer riding slowly by the side, making more serious reflections, as he journeyed, in that short space of time than he had done in the whole course of his previous life. Yes, the merry Willie Sawyer was grave, almost sorrowful when in the early evening he saw the body of the man he had so often tormented deposited on a bed in his town-house.

CHAPTER XI.

Summer with all its charms had passed, the cheerful songs of birds—the lowing of the herds—the gathering in of the harvest, and the pleasures and pastimes of that joyous season had all gone, and Winter returned again as Winter will. Brewster slept in the vault of a London church, and Mabel was free from his importunities and his persecutions. Brewster's patients missed him not, for long ere he died his mad vagaries had lost him all his practice, much to the advantage and profit of Doctor Jenkins.

Brewster's man servant, Thomas, had been hunted down by a distant relative of his late master, who had taken possession of all his effects—and was hanged for his brutal conduct and the robbery he had perpetrated, most of the valuables he had taken having been sold, and the proceeds dissipated in drink and debauchery.

Billy, with his fiery head of hair, had constant opportunities of seeing and making love to Mabel's maid—and one fine morning having obtained a holiday from his master, and being permitted to ride one of his horses, forthwith proceeded to Mrs. Silverton's country house—and boldly made the fair young woman an offer of his hand and heart, upon which he first received a box on the ear, and then ran round the kitchen table offering him a kiss the next time if he could catch her, which Billy did, and received the promised kiss, as well as the further promise of being his wife.

At this period of our history, Billy had been married about two months, and Jenkins had given him the means of furnishing a chemist's shop, and from the high esteem in which Jenkins held him, he was likely to do a prosperous business.

Mabel was once more installed in her town house. All her fears and anxieties had vanished with the untimely death of her persecutor, and as she sat in her room by the cheerful blaze of the fire with the afternoon's sun shining upon the window, she looked the picture of contented happiness. The bloom upon her cheeks was delicate and pure, and her pretty white hands were busy upon a piece of fancy work. Her amiable step-daughter, sat drowsily nodding over a book she had been reading, with her small cur curled up on her lap.

Mabel had been greatly shocked when informed of the miserable ending of Brewster's life, and she wept many tears, for she did not forget some kindnesses he had bestowed upon her : although she knew not at the time they were done for a purpose of his own.

Ten days had passed since the anniversary of her husband's death. With his usual thoughtfulness and kindness of heart, Jenkins had absented himself from her presence, doing violence to his own feelings, so that he might give Mabel time to muse, uninterruptedly and undisturbed, over the memory of the past. She fully understood what had caused his absence, and as fully appreciated, honored and loved him for his delicate reserve.

On the day of which we have spoken, he was with Mabel both in heart and mind, and was approaching the house. Mabel's ear caught the sound of his foot-step upon the stairs, and in a moment after he had entered her room—his face lighted up with the evident joy of his heart. The amiable spinster was roused by his entrance, but she looked at him with scorn and bitterness, exclaiming as she hastily rose from her seat :—

"Curled and gaudy man!" and she and her dog bounced out of the room much to the pleasure both of Mabel and her visiter.

Jenkins laughed and so did Mabel. But after a moment they both became grave, but not sad. Jenkins made two or three hems! as he cleared his throat as if for the purpose of singing one of his pleasant songs, and drew his chair close beside Mabel, much in the same way as Brewster had been accustomed to do soon after old Silverton's death. She trembled, but not as she had been accustomed to tremble—he took her hand, which she did not attempt to withdraw.

"Do you remember, Mrs. Silverton, a walk in the lane near your country house, which we took together some year or more since."

"I do."

"Do you remember also the conversation that passed between us on that particular occasion ? "

"I do."

"And will you now give an answer to the request I made ? "

"What was it ? " said Mabel faintly, " I quite forget."

"Never mind, the precise nature of the request, but will you now say *yes* without further enquiry ? "

"Yes," said Mabel her cheeks and neck covered with blushes and rising.

Not another word was said, and Jenkins also rose : he caught Mabel in his arms, and his lips went so close to hers that had the amiable step-daughter been present she would have felt scandalized at what she would have undoubtedly declared to have been a kiss—and so it was:—

The next morning Mabel and her step-daughter were seated, the one at her book the other at her fancy work, the spinster moody as was her wont, and the widow as happy, or more happy than she ever dreamed of being. She had not told the old maid of her engagement to Jenkins, but had kept the whole happiness it imparted within her own breast. As on the previous day their room was invaded but this time by Willie Sawyer who came in singing more gaily and with greater strength of voice than he had ever done before. Up jumped the spinster, seizing her dog, and intending to leave the room.

"What my darling virgin, leave the room, just as the man who loves you to distraction enters," and he seized her by the arms.

"Come, best foot foremost, and bad's the best —come let's have a dance—now for it, dog and all," and away he whirled and twisted. The poor spinster screaming, and the dog barking, and the more she urged him to desist, the more he whirled her hither and thither, till at length he was obliged to stop from mere exhaustion. He let go his hold of her arms, and threw himself into a chair scarcely able to breathe, at the same time taking the spinster by the waist and pulling her on his knee, and by sheer force keeping her there. She was equally exhausted, and sat panting and passive, unable to offer resistance.

"Now, my sweet angel," gasped out Willie, " do you know why you have danced so gaily ? —eh ; my precious one ! I'll tell you—it was all in honor of Mabel's coming wedding ! She's going to be married to that best of all good fellows Peter Jenkins, and my old darling, we will have lots of dancing on the wedding day—and as I know you are desperately fond of your present partner we will be engaged for the party—and we'll have many a practice beforehand."

The spinster, having recovered her breath, struggled and shouted to the dog's accompanying yells.

"Let me go—let me go—you man of infamy!"

"Not just yet my darling," said Willie, giving her a somewhat tight tug round her waist.

"Let me go, monster! If what this brute says be true, Mrs. Silverton, you ought to blush for your want of proper decorum."

"If it be true," roared Willie.

"Yes, if it be true," screamed the old maid, "but I can't believe in such profligacy!"

"It's as true as gospel," said Sawyer, "and where's the profligacy, my sweet dove, in marrying one of the most honest, upright men in the city of London, and what's more my angelic beauty, one of the handsomest fellows in or out of the city. Isn't it jolly? Suppose, now, my divinity, as I am almost as loveable, and handsome as Peter, and am as fair as the morning, and as neat a little fairy as ever danced by the light of the moon, and have neither vinegar nor sugar in my composition, suppose we get married at the same time—what a beautiful couple we shall make, the admiration of all lookers on—say, my Princess, will you be mine? I positively can't live without you."

He again gave the old maid a hearty squeeze and kissed her, and laughed till fearing she might have a fit from rage he let her go, and the moment she was at liberty she made a dart at his face and kicked his shins, making him laugh to such an extent that he was unable to defend himself. At that moment in walked Jenkins, whom the maiden lady no sooner saw than she left Sawyer, and rushing up to the new comer gave him a tremendous blow in the face with her outspread palm, and dashed out of the room, entered her own, and finished by a flood of tears.

" By Jove ! Peter, you saved me a thrashing. The phial of wrath was giving me a thorough beating."

" And you deserved it, Willie " said Mabel laughing.

That morning everything was arranged for the marriage of Mabel and her faithful reliant lover. Not without a hundred interruptions and suggestions by the merry, happy, Willie Sawyer.

CHAPTER XII.

The year of widowhood as we have said was over, the black dress still worn, but the widow's cap was no longer seen, and the luxuriant hair in all its glossiness and profusion adorned the classically formed head of the pretty Mabel, who whilst looking to the future, spread so bright and happy before her, cherished the past as a pleasing memory.

Her husband's precepts, first taught when, as a child, she sat on a little stool at his feet, took deep root in her heart, and as she advanced to womanhood had been her guide during the short period of her married life, and were still to be her rule.

Mabel was about to take fresh duties upon herself, more arduous than any she had hitherto been called on to fulfil. The world, with its allurements was almost unknown to her, so quietly and so peacefully had her days glided by. Now she was about to enter on a different existence. Her circle of friends had been exceedingly limited hitherto, but, as the wife of a distinguished physician, that circle would be considerably extended, and the duties of society would be as new as they would be strange to her:—

Mabel was timid, and as she reflected on all she would be called upon to undertake, she feared lest she should fail. Her late husband had been always at her side to act for her, and to think for her; but when she became the wife of another, her position would be very different. Jenkins would love and cherish her fondly; he would surround her with every comfort and every luxury, but he could not be always with her. To him she must be something more than a loving wife, she must be the principal ornament to his home, the cheerful, graceful entertainer of his friends, she must not merely be the comforter of her husband's weary hours, she must support his popularity and bring no discredit on his taste in selecting her for a wife.

As all these thoughts arose, Mabel became nervous and bewildered, and almost wished that Jenkins could be induced to quit his profession and live with her the existence she had hitherto led. Still she knew it could not be, and though Mabel feared and trembled she resolved resolutely to fit herself for her task. Two motives would lure her unflinchingly forward—love for the living, and the determination to shew herself the faithful disciple of one who would smile on and bless her from his heavenly home.

Some of these perplexities were imparted to Jenkins, who laughed as he told her she was too pretty not to be admired, and in his eyes every thing she did would be wisest, discretest, best; but when he saw the tears spring to her eyes he became seriously tender, and promised all kinds of loving care.

As soon as the young widow's marriage with Jenkins was arranged, Barbara wrote to her uncle, giving him her version of the whole affair, telling of Doctor Brewster's sad state, into which he had been driven by disappointment; for that her step-mother had at one time never been easy unless he came every day to see her, and, when she had completely bewitched him, turned him off, and was now going to be married to a spendthrift, who would soon scatter the money her father had saved, amongst jews and gamblers. That live any longer under the same roof with Mabel she certainly would not, and she wished her uncle to know her determination. She, however, did not add to her confidential communications her intention as to her future home.

This letter was received by Mr. Silverton, but it failed in creating the anger in his mind the writer had hoped. He knew his niece, and some years back had witnessed much of her temper and unfeminine conduct; but he was not prepared for the early marriage of his brother's widow, though he had felt sure, one so pretty and graceful, and amiable, would ultimately make a second choice. The only remark he made after reading Barbara's letter, was " that he liked the poor little thing, and if she was going to throw herself away on a scamp he was sorry, and would save her if he could. At any rate he would write, warn, and expostulate."

Before, Mr. Silverton could execute his resolve he received a letter from Mabel, telling, in
her simple unaffected manner, the intelligence
previously conveyed to him by Barbara, but
giving a totally opposite colouring to the
affair. Mabel asked her late husband's brother
to be her friend and adviser, and to act for
her, earnestly entreating him to come to her
that he might become acquainted with Doctor
Jenkins.

Though an unfortunate difference of opinion
in their religious feelings had separated the
two brothers, death had swept away all angry
feeling on the part of Mr. Silverton, and he
at once resolved to prove his regard and affection for his departed brother, by doing everything in his power to serve his widow. He
liked a visit to London now and then, and
Mabel's letter gave him an excuse for gratifying his love of change. When he mentioned
his intention to his wife, she smiled, as he

declared " that reluctant, as he was to leave
home he must go, he could not refuse such an
entreaty," but she prudently said nothing;
except that she hoped everything that happened, would tend to Mabel's happiness, and
that the change would increase the comfort of
Barbara: at the same time she gave her
husband to understand, that she would not
receive her niece into her household, for she
disliked all people who professed so much
religion without acting up to their professions,
and Barbara she said was one of these; "her
religion, instead of bringing out kind and
charitable feelings, had made her selfish and
self-righteous."

Mrs. Silverton would have continued edifying
her husband, had he not reminded her of the
necessity of packing his portmanteau and
looking to the buttons on his shirts, whilst he
was gone to give directions to his bailiff, and

to look after sundry other matters that re
quired his attention before leaving home.

Mabel was greatly pleased to see Mr. Silverton, and gave him such a cordial reception,
looking so really handsome as she thanked him
for coming, that he was won over to her side
at once, and Barbara's sarcastic and illnatured
inuendos lost all effect upon him. Mabel
spoke feelingly, and almost reverently of her
husband's death, and her consequent loneliness; of Brewster and his persecutions; and
lastly, with many blushes, of Doctor Jenkins
and his extreme goodness. "I fear," she said
at length, "you will think me precipitate in
marrying a second time, so soon after my dear
husband's death. I confess that I have, myself,
had many scruples on the subject, and
one of my great objects in wishing to see you,
was to ask your candid opinion. Do you
think I shall be shewing disrespect to the one

who is gone. He was ever so kind and considerate; and all of good that I possess I owe to his precepts, and I would not for the sake of gratifying any selfish feeling do anything to shame his teaching. Do you, his brother, speak for him."

"My dear Mabel," said Mr. Silverton considerably affected by her simple and touching appeal, "listen to me a few minutes, and I will not only speak for my poor brother, but in his own words. I had a letter from him when he was first taken ill, in which he told me he had a foreboding that he should not recover. He expressed much anxiety about you, told me about his will, and his words were " what I leave to my dearly loved wife, I bequeath without any reservation. Barbara is amply provided for, and therefore Mabel's portion is for her sole benefit, and to be disposed of as she pleases. I wish her to marry again, and that as soon as her grief for my loss has abated, for I feel certain she will not forget me, even though she learns to love another more passionately than she has ever loved me. I wish you to tell her this, and give her the enclosed letter; but be silent until she informs you of her intention of marrying again, then let her know what I have written, and give her my letter and along with it my blessing. She is too pure to love a bad man, and will be rich enough to marry a poor one."

"Having said thus much, your question I think is fully answered—and it is needless for me to add more. I shall, however, assume a duty and look to your future. I shall see Doctor Jenkins, and find out if he will be likely to take good care of you, if I let you place yourself in his power."

Mabel's tears had been falling fast, as she listened to what seemed like words from the tomb; but as her brother-in-law ceased speaking, a glow of pride suffused her cheeks, as she said :—

"To-morrow you shall see Doctor Jenkins, and I have no fear but that, like your poor brother, when you talk with him you will be perfectly satisfied with his sincerity and nobleness. But please give me my letter. I am indeed anxious to read what my husband wrote ; I always obeyed his advice whilst living, and his words now shall not be unheeded."

"There is the letter," said Mr. Silverton handing it to her, "I will leave you to it's perusal. So good night."

Alone in the sanctuary of her bed-room Mabel broke the seal. She did so tremblingly, but firmly resolved to be guided in her future course by its contents. She knew her late husband's noble nature too well to suppose he would demand the giving up what was now her most cherished hope ; still, she became greatly agitated—as if she feared she knew

not what, but after a minute's pause she un-
folded the paper, and the reader must guess
what were Mabel's feelings as she perused the
following lines :—

" My dearest Mabel,

" The event of this morning has roused long
dormant feelings in my breast, and an action
I begun to think fully justified, is now regarded with self-accusation and almost shame;
Whilst I live I can never tell, how much I
wronged you in asking you to become my
wife. I own I was selfish, but when you left
school and came to reside under my roof, sun
shine and happiness came with you, for my
daughter Barbara's peculiar characteristic
qualities are not such as tend to make a
happy home. My life had passed wearily,
and without an interest beyond the looking
after my worldly affairs. You brought me

social happiness which I cherished, and regard-
less of the injury I did to one I loved better
than life, I asked you to become my wife,
when you were little more than a child, and
you consented to wed a man to whom you
had always yielded obedience, and to whom
you feared to say 'no.' I kept you secluded
from the world and persuaded myself I did
right, but I now feel that I was intensely selfish. I feared your being seen, because I knew
you would be admired, and, when known,
loved. I never took into consideration how
incompatible with your age was the life you
passed with me and Barbara, or, when such
ideas forced themselves upon me, I stifled
them by persuading myself, I acted for your
good. When you told me what had passed
this morning in your interview with Doctor
Jenkins, my selfishness was more palpably
brought to my sight. From what I had seen,
and from what I knew of him, I liked him.

I had heard him highly spoken of, and ascertained that such eulogiums were deserved. He had known and learned to love you, and I could but acknowledge how much better suited he is to be your husband than I am.

"My regret, dearest Mabel, is very bitter. You will, I know, forgive me when you read this confession, but you must also attend to my wishes, formed whilst in health, but with the certainty that I shall leave you a young widow.

"When you are about to form new ties, this letter will be given to you, and you will find how much I wish it should be so : how much I should rejoice to have you filling a station, you are formed to adorn—as the wife of a good man ; one sufficiently young to be a fitting companion, to make you a happy wife and mother. That such may be your fate is the earnest wish and solemn prayer of your devoted husband."

Tears fell plentifully upon the paper from Mabel's eyes as she folded it up, and a prayer of deep thankfulness swelled her bosom. The tears were wiped away, and smiles played around her lips as she longed for the morrow, that she might show Doctor Jenkins the letter, and listen to his expressions of satisfaction. Moreover, she felt pleased that she could now yield to the joy of loving, and being loved, without fear of slighting the memory of the dead. Yes, Mabel was very happy.

The next morning, Doctor Jenkins, after a chat with Mabel, and perusing the letter, was introduced to Mr. Silverton, whose approbation he gained, ere many minutes had passed in coversation. Mr. Silverton stated his reasons for coming to London in something of an apologetic manner, as if he feared his doing so might be intrusive. Doctor Jenkins at once silenced these doubts, saying :—

"My dear sir, had not Mabel written, I

should assuredly have felt it my duty to have
done so, because we want you, at least I do.
It is right that you should see the ogre who
is about to devour your sister-in-law. It is
quite proper that some one should attend to
her interests; and who so desirable as yourself. I am a spendthrift, you know : " he said
jokingly, " therefore it is right Mabel's fortune
should be settled on her. Seriously, such an
arrangement is my wish and determination.
I want nothing with my wife but her affection,
I trust to possess that and shall be rich indeed.
I am not too proud to derive advantage from
her wealth, but I will have no power vested in
me beyond acting as her agent. I am to
succeed a good man in the guardianship of a
treasure, and hope to prove worthy of the
trust."

"You are quite right," answered Mr. Silverton, placing his hand on Jenkins' shoulder

I like you for your disinterested resolve. I will at once see my poor brother's lawyer, and when he has filled sufficient parchments, I will give you a wife with all my heart, and a heartfelt blessing as well."

"Thank you," replied Jenkins, "and now say you will dine with me to-day, after which if Mabel will allow us, we will return here for a social cup of tea."

CONCLUSION.

At the expiration of three weeks—after the interview between Mr. Silverton and Jenkins, as recorded in our last chapter—all the requisite parchments were complete, securing to Mabel the whole of the property left her by her late husband. Mr. Silverton having remained in London all the time attending daily at the office of his late brother's solicitor, as well as going occasionally to Doctor Jenkins' house to consult him upon sundry matters concerning the said settlements. He was also in attendance upon Mabel, and ere the three weeks had ended he told her, that the more he saw and heard of Doctor Jenkins, the more inclined he was to think that she had made a most judicious choice, and one that he fully believed would be productive of happiness to them both.

The requisite legal matters having been so satisfactorily arranged, Mr. Silverton said to Mabel:

" I think, now that there exists no further cause for delay, the sooner the wedding takes place the better, and as I have been so much longer away from home than I anticipated, I fear my wife will be anxious for my return."

" Come, pretty coz," said Willie Sawyer, who happened to be present, " don't fix too early a day for I shall require good notice, as I am to take a conspicuous part in the ceremony. Pray make it four days or at most a week."

" I suspect, Willie, you are already in possession of the secret; as Peter and I have fixed this day week for the wedding to be solemnized."

Sawyer sprang from his seat and seized both Mabel's hands; saying:

"By Jove! Mabel, I honour you for your prompt and womanly decision, no beating about the bush, no blushing and mock modesty, but coming to the point like an amiable and sensible woman as you are. By the beard of my grandmother—I beg pardon—my grandfather, I will get myself up for the occasion in a style that shall astonish even my friend Peter; in fact, I shall put that pink of fashion entirely in the background."

At that moment Jenkins entered the room, and having listened to his friend Sawyer's humorous speech, said:

"Upon my word, Sawyer, I shall be delighted to see your "get up," it may afford me some useful hints."

"I shall tremble for the bridesmaids," said Mr. Silverton, smiling.

"Indeed you may," laughed Sawyer, "for I really feel somewhat infected by the marriage mania."

"Well, Willie, it is a pity Barbara, has determined not to be present," said Mabel.

"Yes, by Jupiter! I should more than ever have won her affections. It's her own fault that she does not witness my decided superiority over other exquisites" (with a sly glance at Jenkins), "for there is no telling what might have come to pass—oil and vinegar might have mixed."

"It is better as it is, Willie, you torment poor Barbara fearfully when you get an opportunity," said Mabel, with a shake of the head.

"By Jove! Mabel, I must be off, or I shall be behindhand with my rig out. I must consult tailor, hairdresser—and—the looking-glass," and with a hearty laugh he left the room singing one of his love songs.

" He is a jovial, pleasant fellow," said Mr. Singleton.

" Yes," returned Peter, " he's more ; he is as honest-hearted a fellow as ever lived, for with all his apparent levity he is full of charity towards his poorer fellow-creatures, and a sincere, steadfast friend."

*   *   *   *   *   *

The marriage took place at the end of the week, Willie Sawyer acting as bridegroom's man. Barbara, absenting herself, he was obliged to find some other partner for the dance. As he promised, he was dressed in the height of fashion. He danced, he sang, he ate, and he drank. He flirted with all the young ladies, and was exceedingly kind and attentive to the elders of the party.

*   *   *   *   *   *

Seven years had elapsed and Doctor Jenkins and Mabel were surrounded by a happy progeny. Sawyer was still a bachelor, and their constant and most welcome guest.

Mabel and two of her children were seated in the arbour at their country house, one fine summer afternoon, when all of a sudden the eldest child, a fair, bright-eyed little girl rushed down the path exclaiming, at the top of her voice,

" Here he comes—here he comes ! "

" Well, saucy, little Mabel, what makes you so riotous this morning, eh ? "

" Oh, cousin Willie—dear god-papa, I have been looking out for you ever so long. Oh! I am so pleased you are come," and jumping up into his arms she put her hands round his neck and kissed him repeatedly.

" You'll smother me, you little imp," said Sawyer giving the child a most affectionate hug, "and what's as bad, you'll spoil and rumple my beautiful shirt frill."

" God-papa, god-papa ! " cried the other

child, a fine handsome little boy of about five
years old. " I'm so glad ! "

" What makes you so glad, master Willie ? "
cried Sawyer, taking the little fellow in his
right arm, his god-daughter still in his left,—
" what makes you so glad ? "

" Oh god-papa, because we shall be so
happy—you make us laugh so."

" Suppose I make you cry, instead," and he
took hold of the boy's ear, as he used to take
Mabel's, and pretended to pull it.

The little fellow seized Sawyer's nose,
saying ;—

" I'll make you tell me one of your funny
stories, or I'll pull your nose."

" Fie ! Willie, fie ! cousin Willie doesn't like
rude children," said Mrs. Jenkins.

" Oh ! Mama ! " said the girl, " its not
dear cousin Willie's fault, though dear papa
says he does everything he can to make us

rude, spoilt children! It's very naughty of papa to say so, isn't it, dear god-papa?"

"To be sure it is," said Sawyer putting down the children. "Come, who'll go fishing with me?"

"I will!—I will!" cried both the children excitedly, "its such fun to see you pull the beautiful fish out of the water."

And Sawyer walked, or rather ran away, the children each catching hold of a tail of his coat, laughing heartily at their cousin's frolicsome pranks.

Mabel saw nothing more of either her cousin or the children till tea time. In the interim Jenkins had arrived, and was comfortably seated in his arm chair, as Willie and the children came in with each a basket of fish in their hands.

"Well, Peter, my lad," cried Willie going straight up to his friend, and shaking him heartily by the hand, "we've had capital sport."

"Oh, yes, dear papa," cried both children getting on to their father's knees. "God-papa, has been so funny, telling us such pretty tales, and he's been singing and laughing, and skipping and jumping."

"And fishing," interrupted Sawyer.

"Oh, yes, and fishing—and he caught such beautiful big fish, and all for your supper, he says."

"Yes," laughed Sawyer, winking significantly at Mabel—"and I hope your appetite will be better than it was some seven years ago; when I told you of a certain lady——"

"Who has made me one of the happiest men in the world, thanks to heaven, and your kind offices at the time," said Jenkins.

Mabel, looked lovingly at her husband—for they had indeed lived a life of uninterrupted happiness.

Jenkins made a large fortune by his profession, and was respected by all his patients high and low; especially by the poor.

THE END.

New Novels by Popular Authors.

—o—o—

In 3 Vols., 31s. 6d ,

LITTLE MISS FAIRFAX

BY THE AUTHOR OF " THE SCHOOLMASTER OF ALTON."

" One of those very rare novels that will attract and please all readers."—*Northern Times.*

" 'The Schoolmaster of Alton' displayed both talent and genius, but 'Little Miss Fairfax' is immensely superior."—*Sussex Advertiser.*

" It will ensure for its author a fame that will endure beyond the time when the great bulk of the novels of the last ten years are forgotten."—*Herald.*

Mr. Newby's New Works.

———o—o———

THE MARY IRA:

*Being the Narrative Journal of a Yachting Expedition from Auck-
land to the South Sea Islands in the Year 1866; a Pedestrian
Tour in a new district of New Zealand Bush, and Anecdotes of
Colonial Life.*

By J. K. M.

Illustrated with Sketches taken on the spot.

———

In 3 Vols., 31s. 6d.,

THE WILD GAZELLE:

A NOVEL.

By C. F. ARMSTRONG,

Author of " The Two Midshipmen," " The Cruise of the Daring,"
" Our Blue Jackets," &c.

In 2 Vols., 21s.,

A TERRIBLE WRONG.

By ADA BUISSON.

" We have rarely come across a novel that, taken all in all, so justifies our hearty commendation as a story of great power and interest. The most particular of men may, without fear, permit their wives, and the most conscientious of women, their daughters, to feast on this *bon bouche* of sensation novels."—*The Atlas.*

———

In 3 Vols., 31s. 6d.,

NORTH OF THE TWEED.

By D. CROWBERRY,

" This is a very entertaining and well-written book, full of interesting, descriptive, and amusing incidents."—*Observer.*
" We have been highly amused with this book."—*Athenæum*
" The incidents and adventures that befel the hero of the tale are related in a graphic and racy manner."—*Berwick Warder.*

Mr Newby's New Publications.

30, WELBECK STREET, CAVENDISH SQUARE.

In Demy 8vo., price 14s. (In November).

HISTORY OF IRISH PERIODICAL LITERATURE,

BY

RICHARD ROBERT MADDEN, M.R.I A.,

Author of "Travels in the East," "Lives and Times of the United Irishmen," "Travels in Turkey, Egypt, Nubia, and Palestine," "Memoirs and Correspondence of the Countess of Blessington," &c., &c., &c.

This History of Irish Periodical Literature, the result of arduous labour and research for the past five years, is not a mere catalogue of names, dates, and compendious characteristics of newspapers and magazines, gleaned from published lists, or memoranda furnished by literary men; but an original and extensive Treatise, illustrative, as it professes to be, of the origin, scope, progress, and design of newspapers, magazines, and periodical miscellanies of all kinds worthy of notice, that have been published in Ireland from the latter part of the seventeenth, to the middle of the nineteenth century.

The importance of such a work executed with due care, diligence, truthfulness, and impartiality, must be obvious to all by whom reliable knowledge is desired, of contingencies, conjunctures, and controversies on subjects of great pith and moment, that have engaged public attention in Ireland during a period of nearly two centuries.

It abounds with periodical notices of Irish periodical originators, contributors, and editors, remarkable for their position, influence, ability, or eccentricity, of past or recent times.

DEDICATED BY PERMISSION

TO

SIR MOSES MONTEFIORE, Bart.

In October will be published, price 21s., in one handsome volume,
Imperial 8vo.

A NARATIVE OF A JOURNEY TO MOROCCO,

BY THE LATE

THOMAS HODGKIN, M.D., F.R.G.S., &c., &c.

Illustrated (from his Drawings taken on the spot) with Chromo-
Lithographs, in the best style of the Art,

By DAY and SON (Limited).

A universal desire has been exprsssed by the friends of the late
Dr. Hodgkin to possess a memento of one whose friendship was
so valued during life—whose death has been so lamented.

It is well known that in 1863-4 Dr. Hodgkin attended Sir Moses
Montefiore in his Mission to the Emperor of Morocco. The Notes
and Sketches, taken during the progress through a country but
little known, and therefore imperfectly described, must certainly
prove highly interesting. Dr. Hodgkin's descriptions are truthful, therefore valuable for the purpose intended—a lasting memento. To render the Work still more pleasing to a large circle
of readers, it will be enriched with a medallion portrait of the
much-lamented and talented Author, a photograph of the tomb,
and a portrait of Sir Moses Montefiore, to whom (with his kind
permission) the Narrative will be dedicated.

The friends and admirers of Dr. Hodgkin, who order copies
before the 10th of October, will have their names inserted in
the volume.

In 1 Vol. Price 12s.

ON CHANGE OF CLIMATE,

A GUIDE FOR TRAVELLERS IN PURSUIT OF HEALTH.

By THOMAS MORE MADDEN, M.D., M.R.C.S. Eng.

Illustrative of the Advantages of the various localities resorted to by Invalids, for the cure or alleviation of chronic diseases, especially consumption. With Observations on Climate, and its Influences on Health and Disease, the result of extensive personal experience of many Southern Climes.

SPAIN, PORTUGAL, ALGERIA, MOROCCO, FRANCE, ITALY, THE MEDITERRANEAN ISLANDS, EGYPT, &c.

" Dr. Madden has been to most of the places he describes, and his book contains the advantage of a guide, with the personal experience of a traveller. To persons who have determined that they ought to have change of climate, we can recommend Dr. Madden as a guide."
—*Athe æum.*

" It contains much valuable information respecting various favorite places of resort, and is evidently the work of a well-informed physician."—*Lancet.*

" Dr. Madden's book deserves confidence—a most accurate and excellent work."—*Dublin Medical Review.*

" It cannot but be of much service to such persons as propose leaving home in search of recreation, or a more benign atmosphere. The Doctor's observations relate to the favourite haunts of English inva-lids. He criticises each place *seriatim* in every point of view."—*Reader.*

" We strongly advise all those who are going abroad for health's sake to provide themselves with this book. They will find the author in these pages an agreeable gossiping companion as well as a profes-sional adviser, who anticipates most of their difficulties."—*Dublin Evening Mail.*

" To the medical profession this book will be invaluable, and to those in ill-health it will be even more desirable, for it will be found not merely a guide for change of climate, but a most interesting volume of travel."—*Globe.*

" Dr Madden is better qualified to give an opinion as to the salu-brity of the places most frequented by invalids than the majority of writers on the subject."—*Liverpool Albion.*

" There is something, and a great deal too, for almost every reader in this volume, for the physician, for the invalid, for the historian, for the antiquarian, and for the man of letters. Dr. Madden has rendered a necessary service to the profession and to the public upon the subject under notice."—*Dublin Evening Post.*

" Dr. Madden's work is fraught with instruction that must prove useful both to practitioners and patients who study it."—*Sanders' News Letter.*

" Dr. Madden deserves the thanks of all those persons afflicted with that dire disease, consumption—as well as of those who suffer from chronic bronchitis, asthma, &c. It is the best work on change of cli-mate that has ever been presented to the public."—*Daily Post.*

In 2 Volumes, Octavo, price 21s.

ENGLISH AMERICA IN 1862;

OR

PICTURES OF CANADIAN PLACES AND PEOPLE.

EXHIBITING OUR COLONIAL POSSESSIONS ON THE AMERICAN CON-
TINENT IN THEIR MORAL, SOCIAL, RELIGIOUS, PHYSICAL,
MILITARY, ECONOMICAL, AND INDUSTRIAL ASPECTS,

By SAMUEL PHILLIPS DAY,

Special Correspondent in Canada, of the *Morning Hera'd;*

Author of "Down South ; or Experiences at the Seat of War in
America," &c., &c.

In 1 vol., Post 8vo., Price 10s. 6d.

HEROIC IYDLS,

AND OTHER POEMS,

By WALTER SAVAGE LANDOR.

"These Idyls may take their place with those heretofore given
us by Mr. Landor. Judged of simply by their merits, they compel
that rare admiration which we yield only to noble ideals made pal-
pable by true art. As recent works they claim the tribute of our
wonder, no less than of our delight."—*Athenæum.*

"The same classical feeling which has given a harmony even to
the most fanciful of his 'Imaginary Conversations,' and moulded
the thoughts of an English poet in the lines of Greek simplicity
and beauty, is to be found here, as delicately marked as ever. Few
artists of modern times have taken a larger range, or have carried
out a clearly conceived purpose with a steadier hand. When Mr.
Landor is gone, we shall have lost at once the founder, and almost
the only follower of a peculiar and grand school."—*Saturday
Review.*

"Here we recognise the dignified pathos and tranquil beauty
characteristic of the best of his 'Hellenics.'"—*Reader.*

"Mr. Landor's works, stamped, as they are, with the impress
of high and original intellect, will ensure for him a proud position among the master minds of the period."—*Bell's Messenger.*

"Passages full of vigorous and tender expression, and containing
sentiments and thoughts in accordance with the former works f
the poet."—*Observer.*

"A book of rare merit, containing many passages of singular
power, grace, and freshness of style, which it would be hard to
match in any modern versifier."—*Morning Herald.*

In 2 vols., Post 8vo., Price 21s.

ANECDOTAL MEMOIRS OF ENGLISH PRINCES,

By W. H. DAVENPORT ADAMS.

Author of "Memorable Battles in English History," &c.

"There can be very little doubt of these memoirs being favourably received by the public."—*Observer*.

"Mr. Adams manifests the same tact and discretion which have made his former publications so highly interesting."—*Bell's Messenger*.

"The book will interest the general reader and furnish landmarks for the guidance of the student."—*Morning Post*.

"Mr. Adams has here opened an almost inexhaustible mine of anecdotal wealth. Scattered over the pages of our history anecdotes of the doings of English Princes have hitherto been interesting only, or chiefly, in connection with the era in which the incidents occurred. Mr. Adams has shown that the anecdotes have an interest of their own, apart from their historical connection."—*Morning Herald*.

THE FOURTH EDITION, ILLUSTRATED.

In 1 vol., Post 8vo., Price 7s. 6d.

A NARRATIVE OF ADVENTURES

IN FRANCE AND FLANDERS,

DURING THE LATE WAR,

By CAPTAIN EDWARD BOYS,

ROYAL NAVY.

"Readers will like this curious narrative, which has all the charm of truthfulness, which few writers, excepting De Foe, could have written half so truthfully; and Captain Boys' interesting and patriotic story is all truth in itself."—*Illustrated Times*.

"Many of the events recorded have long since become matters of history; they are, however, so mixed up with personal adventures simple truth conveyed in a simple form, that we read on with unflagging attention."—*Morning Advertiser*.

"Every youth in Her Majesty's dominions should read these adventures."—*Daily Post*.

In 2 vols., 21s.

IL PELLEGRINO;

OR, WANDERINGS AND WONDERINGS,

By CAPTAIN CLAYTON, F.R.G.S., F.S.A.,

Author of "Ubique,"

" To read Captain Clayton's book without hilarity would be impossible to the gloomiest of home-keeping hermits."—*Athenænm.*

"A more lively, racy, rollicking 'pilgrim' than Captain Clayton, it has not been our good fortune to meet for a long time."—*New Monthly* (July).

" The reader is somehow so led on and on by the spirit of the book, that the end is reached almost unawares, and 'Il Pellegrino,' left with a sigh.' "—*Globe.*

" The work is extremely pleasant, chatty, and agreeable."—*Morning Advertiser.*

" 'Il Pellegrino' displays alternate humour and sensible reflections."—*Court Journal.*

" The author was a most thoughtful reasoner on what he observed."—*Observer.*

" The author is a frank, outspeaking gentleman, and the reader will accompany him in his peregrinations with pleasure, whilst those who are going abroad will thank him for the information he affords, and which serves to prepare them for what they will meet with in their travels."—*News of the World.*

Price, 2s. 6d., beautifully illustrated.

THE HAPPY COTTAGE,

A TALE OF SUMMER'S SUNSHINE,

By the Author of "Kate Vernon," "Agnes Waring."

In 1 Vol. 7s. 6d.

ON SEX IN THE WORLD TO COME,

By the Rev. G. HOUGHTON, A.M.

" A peculiar subject ; but a subject of great interest; and in this volume is treated in a masterly style. The language is surpassingly good, showing the author to be a learned and thoughtful man."—*New Quarterly Review.*

THE LITERARY LIFE AND CORRESPONDENCE

OF THE

COUNTESS OF BLESSINGTON,

By R. MADDEN, Esq., F.R.C.S.-ENG.

Author of "Travels in the East," "Life of Savonarola," &c.

"We may, with perfect truth, affirm that during the last fifty years there has been no book of such peculiar interest to the literary and political world. It has contributions from every person of literary reputation—Byron, Sir E. Bulwer, who contributes an original Poem, James, D'Israeli, Marryatt, Savage Landcr, Campbell, L. E. L, the Smiths, Shelley, Jenkyn, Sir W. Gell, Jekyll, &c., &c. ; as well as letters from the most eminent Statesmen and Foreigners of distinction, the Duke of Wellington, Marquis Wellesley, Marquis Douro, Lords Lyndhurst, Brougham, Durham, Abinger, &c."—*Morning Post.*

OUR PLAGUE SPOT.

In connection with our Policy and Usages as regards Women, our Soldiery, and the Indian Empire.

TAORMINA AND OTHER POEMS.

"It is written with a rare mixture of spirit and grace, and bears the marks of a highly cultivated mind, enriched by travel and by classic lore."—*Scotsman.*

DRAWING-ROOM CHARADES FOR ACTING,

By C. WARREN ADAMS, Esq.

"A valuable addition to Christmas diversions. It consists of a number of well-constructed scenes for charades."—*Guardian.*

In 1 Vol., post 8vo., plates, price 10s. 6d.

DEAFNESS AND DISEASES OF THE EAR;

The Fallacies of present treatment exposed and Remedies suggested from the experience of half-a-century,

By W. WRIGHT, Esq.,

Surgeon Aurist (by Royal Sign Manuel), to Her Majesty, the late Queen Charlotte, &c.

In 1 Vol., price 5s.

FISHES AND FISHING,

By W. WRIGHT, Esq.

" Anglers will find it worth their while to profit by the author's experience."—*Athenæum.*

"The pages abound in a variety of interesting anecdotes connected with the rod and the line. The work will be found both useful and entertaining to the lovers of the piscatory art."—*Morning Post.*

In 1 Vol. £1 1s. Second Edition.

ILLUSTRATED WITH FIFTY-FOUR SUBJECTS BY GEORGE SCHARF, JUNR.

THE MANNERS AND CUSTOMS OF THE GREEKS.

By THEODORE PANOFKA, of Berlin.

The *Times* says: "This new publication may be added to a series of works which honorably characterize the present age, infusing a knowledge of things into a branch of learning which too often consisted of a knowledge of mere words, and furnishing the general student with information which was once exclusively confined to the professed archæologist. As a last commendation to this elegant book, let us add that it touches on no point that can exclude it from the hands of youth."

"It will excellently prepare the student for the uses of the vases in the British Museum."—*Spectator.*

"Great pains, fine taste, and large expense are evident. It does infinite credit to the enterprising publisher."—*Literary Gaze.te.*

In 1 Vol. 14s.

THE AGE OF PITT AND FOX,

By the Author of "Ireland and its Rulers."

The *Times* says : "We may safely pronounce it to be the best text book that we have yet seen of the age which it professes to describe."

"It is a noble work."—*Quarterly Review.*

"It is a powerful piece of writing."—*Spectator.*

In 1 Vol., price 5s.

KNIGHTS OF THE CROSS,

By Mrs. AGAR.

"Nothing can be more appropriate than this little volume, from which the young will learn how their forefathers venerated and fought to preserve those places hallowed by the presence of the Saviour."—GUARDIAN.

"Mrs. Agar has written a book which young and old may read with profit and pleasure."—SUNDAY TIMES.

"It is a work of care and research, which parents may well wish to see in the hands of their children."—LEADER.

"A well written history of the Crusades, pleasant to read and good to look upon."—CRITIC.

In 3 Vols., demy 8vo. £2 2s.

THE HISTORY OF THE PAPAL STATES,

By JOHN MILEY, D.D.,

Author of "Rome under Paganism and the Popes."

"Dr. Miley supports his position with a plentitude and profundity of learning, a force and massive power of reasoning, a perspicuity of logical prowess, and a felicity of illustration rarely met in combined existence amongst historians of any age."—MORNING POST.

"Illustrated by profound learning, deep thought, refined taste, and great sagacity."—DUBLIN REVIEW.

"We have no hesitation in recommending these volumes as characterized by learning, eloquence, and original research."—DAILY NEWS.

In 1 Vol. 10s. 6d.

A HISTORY OF THE KINGS OF JUDAH.

By LADY CHATTERTON.

" No Protestant family should be without this excellent work."
—NEW QUARTERLY REVIEW.

In 1 Vol., demy 8vo., price 12s.

THE SPORTSMAN'S FRIEND IN A FROST,

By HARRY HIEOVER.

" Harry Hieover's practical knowledge and long experience in field sports render his writings ever amusing and instructive. He relates most pleasing anecdotes of flood and field, and is well worthy of study."—THE FIELD.

"There is amusement as well as intelligence in Harry Hieover's book."—ATHENÆUM.

In 1 Vol., price 5s.

THE SPORTING WORLD,

By HARRY HIEOVER.

" Reading Harry Hieover's book is like listening lazily and luxuriously after dinner to a quiet, gentlemanlike, clever talker."
—ATHENÆUM.

" It will be perused with pleasure by all who take an interest in the manly games of our fatherland. It ought to be added to every sportsman's library."—SPORTING REVIEW.

Fourth Edition. Price 5s.

THE PROPER CONDITION OF ALL HORSES,

By HARRY HIEOVER.

" It should be in the hands of all owners of horses."—BELL'S LIFE.

" A work which every owner of a horse will do well to consult."
—MORNING HERALD.

" Every man who is about purchasing a horse, whether it be hunter, riding-horse, lady's palfry, or cart-horse, will do well to make himself acquainted with the contents of this book."—SPORTING MAGAZINE.

In 1 Vol., demy 8vo., price 12s.

SPORTING FACTS AND SPORTING FANCIES,

By HARRY HIEOVER,

Author of "Stable Talk and Table Talk," "The Pocket and the Stud," "The Hunting Field," &c.

"This work will make a valuable and interesting addition to the sportsman's library."—BELL'S LIFE.

"In addition to the immense mass of practical and useful information with which this work abounds, there is a refreshing buoyancy and dash about the style, which makes it as attractive and fascinating as the pages of the renowned Nimrod himself."—DISPATCH.

———

In 1 Vol., price 5s.

HINTS TO HORSEMAN,

SHOWING HOW TO MAKE MONEY BY HORSES,

By HARRY HIEOVER.

"When Harry Hieover gives hints to Horsemen, he does not mean by that term riders exclusively, but owners, breeders, buyers, sellers, and admirers of houses. To teach such men how to make money is to impart no valueless instruction to a large class of mankind. The advice is frankly given, and if no benefit result, it will not be for the want of good counsel."—ATHENÆUM.

"It is by far the most useful and practical book that Harry Hieover has written"—EXPRESS.

———

In 1 Vol., price 10s. 6d.

GHOST STORIES,

By CATHARINE CROWE,

Author of "Night Side of Nature."

"Mrs. Crowe's volume will delight the lovers of the supernatural, and their name is legion."—MORNING POST.

"These Tales are calculated to excite all the feelings of awe, and we may say of terror, with which Ghost Stories have ever been read."—MORNING ADVERTISER.

In 1 Vol., post 8vo., price 5s.

SPIRITUALISM AND THE AGE WE LIVE IN,

By Mrs. CROWE,

Author of "The Night Side of Nature," "Ghost Stories," &c.

In 1 Vol. 10s. 6d.

SKETCHES FROM NATURE & JOTTINGS FROM BOOKS,

By W. H. C. NATION,

Author of "Cypress Leaves," "Trifles."

"The author treats of a variety of subjects connected with the manners and habits of modern life in a humourous spirit."— LONDON REVIEW.

In 1 Vol., 8vo.

A HISTORY OF THE MODERN MUSIC OF WESTERN EUROPE,

FROM THE FIRST CENTURY OF THE CHRISTIAN ERA TO THE PRESENT DAY,

WITH EXAMPLES AND AN APPENDIX EXPLANATORY OF THE THEORY OF THE ANCIENT GREEK MUSIC,

By G. R. KIESWITTER.

With Notes by R. MULLER.

"Herr Kieswitter writes clearly because he sees clearly."— ATHENÆUM.

In 1 Vol. Price 1s. 6d.

THE FIRST LATIN COURSE,

By Rev. J. ARNOLD.

"For beginners, this Latin Grammar is unequalled."— SCHOLASTIC.

In 1 Vol. 5s. Second Edition.

THE ROCK OF ROME,

By the late J. SHERIDAN KNOWLES,

Author of "Virginia," &c.

"Mr. Knowles appears to be only a believer in his Bible, as he comes forward in this work with an earnestness which all true-hearted men will appreciate."—EXAMINER.

"It is a vivid and eloquent exposure of the lofty pretensions of the Church of Rome."—MORNING HERALD.

"It should be in the libraries of all Protestants."—MORNING POST.

In 3 Vols. Price £2 14s.

A CATHOLIC HISTORY OF ENGLAND,

By W. B. MAC CABE, ESQ.

"This work is of great literary value."—TIMES.

"A better book, or more valuable contribution to historical literature, has never been presented to the reading public."—OBSERVER.

"A valuable and extraordinary work."—QUARTERLY REVIEW.

Dedicated, by permission, to EARL GRANVILLE, Lord President of the Committee of Council on Education.

Price 2s. plain, and 2s. 6d. gilt edges.

"OLD SAWS, NEWLY SET."

"Earl Granville's recognition of this little book is a certain guarantee of its usefulness and ability. It will cause delight to thousands of young hearts, as well as give a moral tone to thousands of young minds. As a book for schools, and for families educated at home, we can affirm there have been few books published of greater value."—DAILY POST.

"The efficacy and attractiveness of allegory as a means of illustrating great moral truths have been acknowledged in all ages, and Mr. George Linley's genius has done good service in publishing this 'new version of old fables.' This new setting of old saws is well timed and appropriate. Mr. Linley's view is graceful and melodious, and, while he tells his familiar stories in a gay and easy manner, he takes care to point their moral with a piquancy and precision not to be misunderstood."—MORNING POST.

Fourth Edition. 4s.

THE BEE-KEEPER'S GUIDE,

By J. H. PAYNE. Esq.

"The best and most concise treatise on the management of bees."—QUARTERLY REVIEW.

•

In 1 Vol. 5s.

STEPS ON THE MOUNTAINS.

"This is a step in the right way, and ought to be in the hands of the youth of both sexes."—REVIEW.

"The moral of this graceful and well-constructed little tale is, that Christian influence and good example may have a better effect in doing the good work of reformation than the prison, the treadmill, or either the reformatory."—CRITIC.

"The Steps on the Mountains are traced in a loving spirit. They are earnest exhortations to the sober and religious-minded to undertake the spiritual and temporal improvement of the condition of the destitute of our lanes and alleys. The moral of the tale is well carried out; and the bread which was cast upon the waters is found after many days, to the saving and happiness of all therein concerned."—ATHENÆUM.

In 2 Vols. Price 10s.

SHELLEY AND HIS WRITINGS,

By C. S. MIDDLETON, Esq.

"Never was there a more perfect specimen of biography."—WALTER SAVAGE LANDOR, ESQ.

"Mr. Middleton has done good service. He has carefully sifted the sources of information we have mentioned, has made some slight addition, and arranged his materials in proper order and in graceful language. It is the first time the mass of scattered information has been collected, and the ground is therefore cleared for the new generation of readers."—ATHENÆUM.

"The life of the Poet which has just appeared, and which was much required, is written with much beauty of expression and and clearness of purpose. Mr. Middleton's book is a masterly performance."—SOMERSET GAZETTE.

"Mr. Middleton has displayed great ability in following the poet through all the mazes of his life and thoughts. We recommend the work as lively, animated, and interesting. It contains many curious disclosures."—SUNDAY TIMES.

Price 1s. 6d.

PRINCE LIFE,

By G. P. R. JAMES, Esq.,

Author of "The Gipsy," "Richelieu," &c.

"It is worth its weight in gold."—THE GLOBE.

"Most valuable to the rising generation; an invaluable little book."— GUARDIAN.

In 2 Vols. £1 1s. cloth.

THE LIFE OF PERCY BYSSHE SHELLEY,

By CAPTAIN MEDWIN,

Author of "Conversations with Lord Byron."

"This book must be read by every one interested in literature."—MORNING POST.

"A complete life of Shelley was a desideratum in literature, and there was man so competent as Captain Medwin to supply it."—INQUIRER.

"The book is sure of exciting much discussion."—LITERARY GAZETTE.

In 1 Vol. 10s. 6d.

ASHTON MORTON,

A NOVEL.

" Both honest and well meant. Its pages do not contain the faintest suggestion of 'sensationalism.' They breathe throughout an air of genuine, every-day religion."—ATHENÆUM.

"The author has evidently sketched her *dramatis personæ* from life ; her models have been carefully and judiciously chosen. We heartily commend ' Ashton Morton' to the perusal of those who desire to meet in the pages of fiction characters and incidents of every day life. There are many characters in it it will not be easy to forget."—PUBLIC OPINION.

In Three Vols.

MAGGIE LYNNE,

By ALTON CLYDE,

Author of " Tried and True," &c.

" There are many characters of interest in the novel, and the various scenes are written with talent."—OBSERVER.

"We can honestly praise this novel."—MANCHESTER GUAR-DIAN.

" A story of strong character and deep domestic sympathies. No novel reader will be able to lay down these volumes till ' Maggie Lynne' has become Mrs. Paul Dillon. We have not lately taken up a work which is better calculated to wile away a quiet afternoon."—MORNING ADVERTISER.

" Sound in tone, enforcing by precept and example sentiments which are calculated to produce salutary effects on the mind of the young."—BIRMINGHAM ADVERTISER.

" There are few writers of fiction who have trespassed so near to the ' wild and thrilling' incidents of the ' legitimate' novel with the same clever avoidance of what is unreal and inartistic as the author of ' Tried and True,' in his present work ' Maggie Lynne.' Where many have failed, the author of ' Maggie Lynne' has secured a fairly earned triumph. The diction is pure, the characters natural, and the construction of the plot clever ; it is no wonder then that the author has succeeded in making ' Maggie Lynne' at once a charming and entertaining novel."—PUBLIC OPINION.

" The author shows constructive power and much cleverness in the delineation of character, with an easy, agreeable style."—SHARPE'S MAGAZINE.

In 1 Vol. 10s. 6d.

ADVENTURES OF A SERF'S WIFE

AMONG THE MINES OF SIBERIA.

"In this volume the reader will find a very graphic and truthful idea of the physical condition of a large portion of Russia and its people."—OBSERVER.

"A better idea of the inner parts of Russia may be derived from reading this single volume than from any works of travel."—LONDON REVIEW.

"The story is of deep interest, while the charming sketches of Russian peasant life are deserving of great praise."—PUBLIC OPINION.

"'The Serf's Wife' might aspire to be reckoned among works of history."—CHURCH AND STATE REVIEW.

In 3 Vols. 31s. 6d.

THE GAIN OF A LOSS.

A NOVEL.

By the Author of "The Last of the Cavaliers."

"The story is well told, and the suspense, the constant change from hope to despair at first, and the final triumph of despair forms a most touching part in this history of a true and faithful love."—OBSERVER.

"The author of 'The Last of the Cavaliers' is known to a numerous body of readers, and this new book, so far from disappointing her friends, will give them additional pleasure and fresh reasons for their admiration of a truly talented writer."—MANCHESTER GUARDIAN.

"An excellent novel, in every way worthy of the reputation of the author of 'The Last of the Cavaliers.' For grace, delicacy, and dramatic skill, we have read few things so good in the novels that have recently been in our hands."—LONDON REVIEW.

"The book is pervaded by an excellent spirit."—ATHENÆUM.

In 3 Vols. 31s. 6d.

A TROUBLED STREAM.

By the Author of "The Cliffords of Oakley."

"The story is told with much taste."—BELL'S MESSENGER.

"It is a pretty story."—OBSERVER.

FOURTH EDITION.

In Three Vols.

C O M M O N   S E N S E .

A NOVEL.

By the Author of "Trodden Down."

"To read common sense in a novel is a very uncommon thing, but to find three volumes of common sense is perfectly surprising; yet such is the case with Mrs. Newby's last work. Every chapter contains an instructive lesson in life, an object set before us to acquire, and the means of obtaining it by the most upright and honourable means. It may with safety be recommended as an admirable novel."—OBSERVER.

"We have read this novel with pleasure It is a healthy, sensible, and interesting story The title is sober, and scarcely indicates the high order of qualities which are illustrated in the narrative—a story which may be read with profit as well as pleasure."—ATHENÆUM.

"We predicted that 'Kate Kennedy' would be the precursor of still higher achievements, and we have not been disappointed. It can with advantage be put into the hands of the youngest novel reader, who may learn from it that the smallest affairs in life may be regulated by the highest principles."—VICTORIA MAGAZINE.

"The whole tone of the book is healthy, the style is easy, and the language well chosen. The love scenes are far more true to life than the sickly sentimentalities we are often invited to accept as heart effusions. The story is built on one great evil of the present day, the living beyond one's means, and we would particularly call attention to the good feeling which is shown as existing between the different classes of society. The plot is simple and natural. It is one of the best novels of the day, the healthy tone of which will place it on the same shelf with those of Miss Austen."—READER.

In 2 Vols. (This Day).

THE STORY OF NELLY DILLON,

A Novel.

By the author of "Myself and my Relatives," &c.

In 2 Vols. (This Day).

HETTY   GOULDWORTH,

A NOVEL.

By GEORGE MACAULAY.

In Three Vols.

ALL ABOUT THE MARSDENS.

A NOVEL.

" An interesting story told with truly feminine delicacy. It is sure to become popular."—Observer.

"The reader who can appreciate home details, charming development of loving natures, kindly sympathies, and small errors of the head—but not of the heart—will peruse this work from the commencement to the close with pleasure and profit."—Bell's Messenger.

" An interesting tale of pure domestic life, very pleasantly written, is this story of the 'Marsdens.' Life, its aim and ends, are earnestly dealt with, and grave lessons are thus naturally engendered. It is a perfectly moral and well considered story, and will prove safe and pleasant reading for our young people."—Court Circular.

" Mrs. Waller writes gracefully and agreeably; her characters are true to nature, and carefully drawn. The story is one eminently suited for young lady readers. Nothing can be purer than the tone and teaching of the story."—Sharpe's Magazine.

" It presents talent of no common order."—Public Opinion.

In 3 Vols.

TREASON AT HOME.

A NOVEL.

" It is somewhat remarkable to open a new novel and to find it possesses so much interest and so many striking qualities as ' Treason at Home.' It is written with great ease and power."—Court Circular.

" This is a well written, interesting story, which we can safely recommend. We congratulate the author on her success. Lady Tremyss is a well sketched character, carefully filled in, and the fascination which is intended to surround her is plainly felt by the reader. ' Treason at Home' is a very superior novel."—Observer.

" It is a long time since we have met with a work of fiction possessing so much freshness and originality."—Court Journal.

In Three Vols.

IT MAY BE TRUE.

A NOVEL.

By MRS. WOOD.

" A highly interesting novel."—Observer.

" ' It may be True' is a novel good enough in all respects to warrant us in recommending our readers to read it. It is clever, spirited, sensible, and interesting, and when powerful writing, or vivid description, or genuine humour is wanted Mrs. Wood is equal to all these occasions."—Athenæum.

23

In 3 Vols. 31s. 6d.

THE MAITLANDS.

A NOVEL.

By the author of "Three Opportunities."

"Each chapter is a homily; every volume contains a world of good advice. The strictest parent might rejoice to see his daughter poring over its pages."--LONDON REVIEW.

In 1 Vol. 10s. 6d.

UNCLE CLIVE.

A Novel.

"There is no lack of spirit in this story, and the humourous portions are decidedly good."—ATHENÆUM.
"It will claim more than ordinary attention."—BELL'S MESSENGER.
"It will repay reading."—READER.
"It is decidedly entertaining."—OBSERVER.

In 2 Vols. 21s.

KATE KENNEDY,

By the author of "Common Sense," "Trodden Down," &c.

"There is a freshness in this story which makes the reading of this book a real pleasure. This is one of the few tales that may be put into the hands of the youngest of novel readers with perfect confidence."—VICTORIA MAGAZINE.

"A natural, and let us add an agreeable, surprise will greet the reception of 'Kate Kennedy.' We know of no better mode of describing Mrs. Newby's last effort than by classing it with Miss Mulock's 'Christian's Mistake.' The work is full of that suggestive and pointed conversational writing, which carries the story along."—MANCHESTER GUARDIAN.

"'Kate Kennedy' is worthy of the author of 'Wondrous Strange.' More we cannot say, except that it appears wondrous strange to us that the name of the great unknown should be kept a secret. It is written throughout with good sense, good taste, and good feeling, and abounds in vivid and interesting scenes. The story is admirable, and is put together with unsurpassable art, care, life, and simplicity."—BRIGHTON EXAMINER.

In 2 Vols. (In October).

THE MASTER OF WINGBOURNE,

A NOVEL.

In 3 Vols.

WONDROUS STRANGE,

By the author of "Common Sense," &c.

"We emphatically note the high tone of pure principle which pervades whatever Mrs. Newby writes"—SATURDAY REVIEW.

"Mrs. Newby has made a tremendous rise up the literary ladder in this new and *moral* sensational novel. The interest is so deep and exciting that we read on without noting time till the early hours of morning, and on arriving at the end of this most fascinating fiction, close the volumes, re-echoing the title—Wondrous Strange!" EXPRESS.

In 2 Vols. 21s.

A HEART TWICE WON,

By H. L. STEVENSON.

Dedicated (by permission of his daughter) to her cousin the late W. M. Thackeray.

"The characters are limned with a steady 'pencil, and the colouring dashed in with broad lights"—WORCESTER HERALD.

"A simple story pleasantly told."—BELL'S MESSENGER.

"It will be read with the liveliest interest."—PUBLIC OPINION.

In Three Vols. Price 31s. 6d. (Sept. 25th).

OUR BLUE JACKETS

AFLOAT AND ASHORE.

By C. F. ARMSTRONG,

Author of "The Two Midshipmen," "The Lily of Devon," "The Naval Lieutenant," &c.

In 2 Vols. (In October).

LOST AT THE WINNING POST,

A NOVEL.

By the Author of "A Heart Twice Won."

In 3 Vols. (In November).

NEW NOBILITY,

A NOVEL.